Divine Embrace

PREACHER'S KID SERIES
BOOK TWO

MICHEL PRINCE

EDITED BY
ERIN CRAMER

ILLUSTRATED BY
COVERS IN COLOR

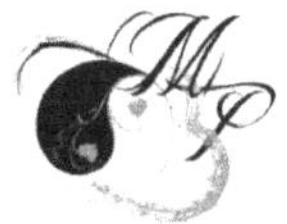

Dearest Divinity,

Any God that says my desire to kiss you is a sin doesn't understand what sin is. And if he does, then I'll accept the damnation.

Yours,
P-

Chapter One

"Vin, I can't believe you're leaving me."

To say my best friend Angela Jefferson was dramatic would be an understatement. Leaving, yes, but it wasn't forever. Three months, nothing more, and it would be a huge boost to my career. That didn't stop her from bursting through my door five minutes ago and singing "Love Don't Live Here Anymore" loud and proud. Anytime I tried to interrupt, she'd rewind to "you abandoned me," ending, of course, in a fainting spell on the couch where her spiral curls now dangled over the arm, her eyes closed, with her forearm across her face as if she could no longer brave the world.

"And yet, you're willing to crash at my condo rent-free while I'm gone."

"Girl, you have a security system that works, not one that glitches if you hit the box right." As she finally righted herself, the dark hazel eyes I'd known since kindergarten smiled behind the obvious sadness. "And underground parking. Please, it's about to be January in Detroit. I may be a fool, but I ain't a damn fool."

Angela and I hadn't been apart for more than a few days since we were five and determined we had to be related because we both had *son* in our last name, her being a Jefferson and me an Anderson—Divinity Anderson, or Vin to those who have known and loved me forever. Five-year-old theories of relationships were predicated on the obscure most days, and yet the weight could last a lifetime. Outside of our love of puzzles, and the fact we both had lost our top front baby teeth the same week so we had matching smiles, we couldn't have been or looked any more different.

While she had the tall, lean model body and dark brown skin, I had a bit more curve to my hip. Far from short, I was average height with a belly crunches couldn't even erase and thighs made for snuggling, not running. My long box braids were currently twisted up into a bun as I taped another box of my "must-haves in Georgia" she would hopefully ship to me later this week.

The timing of this move was perfectly aligned with Angela's lease ending, so she was tossing her big things into a storage unit and had already moved her must-haves into my place. Detroit would always be home, but I had to admit there was a part of me that had wanted to discover Atlanta. The new Elrod Motors plant was going to be built about an hour outside of the city in a medium-sized town with lots of dying little towns within its radius—still considered part of the Atlanta metro area, although it was probably the last ring.

"Committed to the community" would be front and center of the recruitment campaign. Thankfully I wasn't on the meet and greet committee. They were doing permanent transfers, not limited like the one I had as project manager. Up until now I'd been on the strategy team back at the corporate office, with same-day fly in and out to the location to give me a feel of where we'd be building. But we were down to nut-cutting time, and I had to supervise the final construction and setup for the plant.

With me being the third generation of Elrod employees, my family had gone from cleaning crew, to assembly line, to boardroom. Not a bad come-up, though I wish my grandfather could have been the one to smash the glass ceiling and not me. The Big Three car companies had built Detroit, and you found loyalists among the residents. Jokes against the competition were part of core curriculum in school here, with battles ceasing only when union contracts were up for renewal. Then, and only then, did the brotherhood of working men and women dissolve those lines to find common ground.

"Question, you're staying in Atlanta, right?"

"First-ring suburb," I corrected as I headed into my bedroom to continue packing. "Elrod rented part of an apartment building furnished for my team."

"But let's say I come down one weekend. Are they going to rat you out if I steal you away for a night or two?"

"Nefarious intent?" I raised my left eyebrow, knowing

my bestie a bit too well, as I slid the hangers in my closet until I uncovered my old party dresses.

"Is there any other?" she chortled.

"Jesus, I'd have to be poured into this dress." I held the red body-con dress I hadn't worn in at least three years. "And I'd need the Jaws of Life to be removed from it."

"They're called Spanx," Angela said as the back of her hand slapped my tummy. "You're with the company all about form, function, and curves."

Tucking the dress to the back of the closet, I shook my head and went back to the mix of power suits and khakis with logoed polos for when I had to go on-site.

"This is a respite from nefarious activities."

"Damn, woman, when was the last time we had one of those nights?" Angela questioned as she removed a few other dresses, holding them up to my backside. "Not since Terrence broke your heart and you went on a rampage of 'I'm over it' drinking."

"Terrence did not break my heart," I sniped.

"Didn't he?" She slipped a black sequined number off a hanger and began rolling it tightly to stuff in my luggage.

"The man never had it."

"He had something," she countered. "Blackout orgasms."

"I had to black out to achieve an orgasm from a dream man, more likely."

"Jesus, girl, you never give a man a chance." Moving more of my clothes around, she began opening shoeboxes to help find the right heels to send me on my way. "Ever since...well, ever. Boys at school could barely get a dance with you, let alone a date."

"I was focused on my studies," I objected. "Nothing wrong with that. Besides, my parents had finally gotten on the same shift and weren't going to let me have anyone over or let me go anywhere, so what was the point?"

"The point was to rebel."

A smile stretched across her face as she plucked my one extravagance from my closet. Red bottoms. The shoes had no place in my wardrobe, and yet, on an impulse, I'd picked them up. Impractical on so many levels. I lived in the Midwest, which meant our two seasons were winter and construction, so even getting to the car without damaging them was a stretch. Add in the fact I wasn't exactly pulling the type of men to take me to a five-star restaurant even on a sunny day, and I took the box from her to return it to its resting place.

"If you leave those here, I will be wearing them on the regular, like to get coffee or go to the DMV."

"To pay for your hundred or so tickets?"

"Right, I won't be going to the DMV, but you get the idea."

"I'm going to be with a bunch of hicks outside of Atlanta digging in dirt. I don't need them."

A tug-of-war had ensued between the two of us and the box of $1,000 shoes I should have returned the moment I got them. It was an immature purchase made with my first big paycheck after I signed the contract for my job, one that wasn't a simple hourly wage position, but a contracted management one.

"You will be less than a hundred miles from Atlanta." Her hard shove of the box in my hand made me take a step back. "We both know that's like next door in Midwest miles. You can go in town, sit down at a fancy bar all the executives go to after work, and flash a little red bottom to let them know you belong there."

"Or," I said, returning the shove, "I can leave them here and pack a pair of running shoes so I can wear them with a dress that doesn't require that I'm trussed up in binding that will rearrange my internal organs."

"Take the damn shoes, Vin," she growled through gritted teeth.

"A waste of space in my luggage," I groaned.

"Better there than in my closet."

"Oh no, you're staying in the spare bedroom, not mine."

"But I need the southern exposure your room gets in the morning."

"That's north." My finger pointed bluntly out my bedroom window. "And my closet is for my things."

"But is it? Is it really? All I see are mom suits and mementos of clothes that not only time, but you forgot."

"Why are we friends?" I questioned without a hint of malice in my heart.

"Because bodies needed to be buried and you've got that bad back," she teased. "I have an unlimited supply of shovels. It's a symbiotic relationship. You give me closet space, I help you commit felonies."

"Never once have I been charged with a felony."

"Need I say more? No reason to thank me," she beamed, holding up her hands as if she couldn't handle the praise. "It's what I do."

"I'm sure it is."

Angela continued her sort-and-shove method of making room in my closet. Shaking my head, I returned to arranging my bags, thankful I'd be flying first class so I could add an extra forty pounds between the two of them. Using compression bags, I was able to maximize space, as well as get an accurate measurement with my luggage scale before packing fully. Luckily I'd have time to air out and iron when I arrived, a few days of settling in before I took off like a shot. Groceries were being delivered, I had a company car set to pick me up at the airport, and all I had to do was get there.

"Um, Vin, is this a necessity?" Angela asked, shaking an old box decorated with stickers and doodles. "I thought we got rid of this box?"

"Mmmm...did you?"

"Yes, I distinctly remember you running out of a dorm room and tossing the box into a bonfire in a cleansing ritual made up by the Madisons."

The Madisons were a group from college bonded by their first name. Angela and I would make fun of them most days, until she pointed out the fact we had been best friends for over a decade because of our last names. But on one particularly nefarious night, I was lamenting a lost…I couldn't call it a love, and yet, I could. I had dug out my childish box of mementos, mostly letters, and was going to toss Peter Young onto the pyre created by the Madisons with their frat boy fuckups. The gifts and notes, not the actual men, of course, unless you considered the fact that Madison Reynolds had turned a stuffed bear into a voodoo doll in her mind.

Either way, I'd faked a toss onto the fire and then tucked the box back into my bag, successfully hiding it from Angela until today. The judgment in her eyes stung as I snatched the box back and sat at the edge of my bed, my finger absently tracing a flower sticker he'd sent me one time that I had affixed to the lid. Inside this box were dreams of a future that had grown from a writing assignment, pen pals from a school thousands of miles away who told of their lives as we discussed ours. I could still hear Mrs. Conners saying, *"You never know, this person may have a very different life from you, but they could become a lifelong friend. Even if you never meet in real life."*

We'd scoffed at the idea of writing to a stranger and turning them into a friend, and yet there had been a part of me daydreaming about getting letters until I was ninety from my friend in Billingsworth, Georgia. While most of the class never went beyond the three required letters, Peter had slipped an extra piece of paper into the last letter with his real address, and I did the same. Fourth-grade friendship evolved in a way I had never even imagined, bringing me highs unlike any others and lows that shattered me in ways I thought I'd never be able to repair.

Eighteen Years Ago

Hey Divinity,

My teacher said to add my address to this letter if I wanted to continue to get letters from you. I hope you do the same. I don't think I'll ever be a Lions fan, but the Pistons are cool. Mostly I play baseball, though I'm not very good. Guess I need more practice. It's hard when Coach wants to have us at the field and my dad says I have to be at the church for youth group.

Well, I live at 734 Chambers Street, Billingsworth, Georgia. That's GA, and I guess you already know about Billingsworth. Guess I better go now. If your letter has your address, I promise I'll write to you.

I never break promises. That's one thing the Youngs are known for.

Your pen pal,
Peter

Hi Peter,

It seems weird to write Dear even though Mrs. Conners says we're supposed to. I think I'll take the half point and be real with you instead of fake. No reason to stand on ceremony. That's an Anderson saying. At least the Andersons I'm related to. Maybe someday I'll write Dear to a boy, but right now, it's a grandma-type word.

I like the idea of writing outside of class to each other. I know where my parents keep the stamps, so we should be able to do that. I live at 12396 Lexington Way West, Eastpointe, MI 48201. I don't know why I always liked the fact my Eastpointe address has West in it. Am I crazy? Or just a little touched? My great-grandparents were from the South and said that's what you all call the ones who aren't right.

At least that's how my grandmother explains it.

Your friend,
Divinity

I knew when I signed my name I probably should have signed *Your pen pal*, but even through just a few letters, I was already feeling as if Peter was a friend of mine. Over the next few months, I used up all of my mother's stamps and got the hard end of a glare for it. To me, I was keeping myself busy and out of trouble. Her point was to make sure I actually finished a letter or thought instead of realizing I forgot something later and shooting off another envelope. Thanks to after-school chores, I'd earned my own money to get a book of stamps, and I did slow down. Almost to the point I thought he forgot about me, until I got a letter suddenly in seventh grade.

Ten Years Ago

. . .

"I'm sorry, Vin, I can't be your wing man," Angela said as she tousled her hair before putting in tiny butterfly clips to keep it out of her eyes. "Kendra called out, and I'm the only one who can cover her shift."

"Can I use your car at least?" I begged, knowing there was no way I could talk my parents into giving up the keys without explaining where I was going to go. "I have gas money. You know that I was totally filling up your car after."

"Then how would I get home from work?"

"Bus?" I questioned, knowing daggers would soon be shot directly from Angela's eyes to mine. "Maybe you can get a ride from that guy you've been eyeing at the kiosk that sells the helicopter toys."

"Oh, so I'm supposed to go up to a random guy I've been drooling over and never so much as spoke to and ask for a ride?"

"This could be your chance." I grabbed her hands and put on my best puppy dog eye look. "Please, please? I'd say, 'Be my best friend,' but we both know you're that and so much more already."

"Fine, I'll do it, but only because I'm so tired of hearing about this Peter guy that is probably a serial killer, and I want to be on TV when they interview me feigning ignorance. I'll do my best Meryl Streep impression of innocence and confusion at how I thought I was giving in to love and passing my friend the keys to her future." Her eyes narrowed and brow furrowed. "Little did I know she was the final bit he needed to finish the ottoman in his collection of skin-covered furniture."

"The ottoman," I laughed, placing both hands on my hips and turning from side to side. "And here I thought my ass was perfect as a pair of throw pillows."

"Ugh, if you get killed, I'm going to resurrect you and kill you myself again."

"Promise." I extended my pinkie to her, and she locked hers around mine. "He's real and my second-best friend in the world."

"He's a diary entry that responds," she groaned, slapping her car keys into my palm.

The excitement and nerves had even me second-guessing this plan Peter and I had in place, but from the time he told me he would be a counselor at Little Shepherd's Camp in Meadowbrook, Michigan, I knew it might be our only chance to be this close. He'd gone there a few times as a camper when he was younger, but commitments with baseball had kept him from the summerlong sleepaway camp. Having lost the love of the game, he had no excuse and had to go now.

I hadn't so much lied to my parents about my plans for the night. They knew I'd be spending the night at Angela's, and with the two of us, that was standard on the weekends. Most Friday nights we ended up together at one of our houses and didn't leave until Sunday. And I would end the night at Angela's. I'd just have traveled a few hours, now solo, to Nowhere, Michigan, to a camp Peter said was where they molded kids into preachers.

The path his parents had set for him wasn't one that he wanted, but much like with me, he was under their roof and their rules. He said if parents knew what happened after lights-out at Little Shepherd, they probably would burn the place down to exorcise the demons infecting their children.

The hardest part of meeting up with Peter was the fact he didn't talk on the phone. There was something about the letters between us allowing for anticipation and hope to bloom. Now as I was making my way toward the camp, I realized having a cell phone number at the least probably would be important. This was crazy and impulsive. Even with the map I'd reviewed three thousand times since we'd come up with this plan, I couldn't get myself settled enough to think properly. Maybe that was a good thing. Love was one of those things that didn't need an explanation or plan.

They were between sessions, so there was a lull in the adult administrators caring about bed checks and the like. Unlike most summer camps, where the junior counselors would head into the nearest town to get into trouble, at best they'd have a bonfire and discuss the Lord. Peter had written how he thought the camp was indoctrinating when he was ten. It was nothing like being a counselor. While he loved the Lord and believed Jesus was his savior, that didn't mean he agreed with the fire-and-brimstone threats of Hell taught at the camp. For him, you couldn't have a loving God and one that condemned a person for life because they wanted to kiss a girl.

His letter had followed up that remark with how "*I can't imagine a world where the thoughts I have of touching your lips is a sin.*" I'd reread that line a million times at least, closing my eyes as I envisioned him. I swore I could feel him gently bringing his lips to mine, and suddenly it was more than his lips touching me. It was all of him, exploring every part as we fell away into a blissful make out session that went further. There was no fumbling and awkwardness like the one I attempted freshman year with Cameron. Was it sad I wasn't saving myself for Peter and yet I couldn't bring myself to even kiss another boy without thinking of him? Angela said I was too stuck in books to have a good time. For me Peter was perfect. On paper or not, he was who I'd wanted from the moment we both realized cootie shots were bullshit.

After turning down the access road Peter had told me to take, I found the third right and tucked the car right where he'd told me to. In the distance I could see a few brown buildings, but for the most part, I was surrounded by three-story-high trees and nothing more. It was barely seven o'clock, and the sun was nowhere near setting. This was why so much trouble happened in the summertime. If you didn't need to be home until the streetlights came on, and that was at nearly ten thirty at the peak of summer, you had plenty of time to start stuff. Right then, even tucked away deep in the woods, I felt exposed by the bright orb shining bright on its descent to the horizon.

Checking my watch a few times, I flipped the visor down and applied a light lip gloss, closed my eyes, and actually prayed. My family weren't more than High Holy Day church members, but we were to give thanks, and I only felt right to thank God while sitting at this camp.

Stepping out of the car onto the uneven campground, I tugged down my cutoff shorts and immediately was hit by the heat—and the sound of buzzing insects in air that hadn't been filtered through an exhaust manifold. Here I was an hour from the city, and I might as well have been in another world. Michigan was full of harsh contrasts. Coming to the country backwoods area I'd been told wasn't for us made me wonder why not. It was gorgeous outside of the bugs. I should be finding my way to places like this.

Funny how over the years I'd heard it called "God's Country" in the northern part of Michigan, but never truly understood until that moment. The trees were a mix of pine, maple, and poplar. Poplars were my favorite with their hinge-like leaves that rustled more on the end of their stem, not anchored tight, but instead more like a wrist that dangled and rocked. I'd learned about them in elementary school, describing them in detail to Peter, with their silvery green leaves. Only then I couldn't explain how they appeared to flash when they blew in the wind. Even now it was a phenomenon that transfixed me as if they were hypnotizing.

After five minutes my stomach started gurgling. Disembodied voices from camp staff seemed to be coming from every direction as I sat on the hood of Angela's car. My fingers curled under the slight break between the hood and the grill as I closed my eyes, willing Peter to be there when I opened them. Sweat from a mix of heat and nerves trickled down my back, and I could feel it sliding under the waistband of my shorts. Hopping up, I shook out my hands and began talking to myself.

"This is crazy, Vin. Get your ass back in the car, and you'll be able to make it to the mall in time to pick up Angela. Who knows, the helicopter guy could be a serial killer, and you've now damned your best friend all because your dumb ass fell in love with a letter."

"Just a letter?" a male voice said in a southern accent making the word *letter* sound like *lead* and *er*.

Spinning around, I swore I was in a movie. A ray of sunshine broke through the leaves and beamed down where Peter stood. Bits of dust floated in the stream as if glitter was being dropped on him as the crooked smile his mother hated softened his strong jawline. His blondish-brown hair was lighter than the last picture he'd sent me, probably because he'd been out in the sun for weeks now. Then again, it could have been the Heaven-sent aura currently making him glow.

"Now here I thought you'd come to see the guy who writes 'em," he said, and I did my best to swallow back my shock at how tall he was. At least six-one, if not two, with a lean body with a bit of muscle to it, I noticed, as he ran his fingers through the flop of his hair to slick it back.

Jesus, he was real. This wasn't me hearing a voice as I read his letters. The voice was so much better than I'd dreamed. Could a voice be both velvet and sensual? No matter. The reality was my knees were becoming weak and not from the heat. Why hadn't I given him a twang? He was from Georgia and a self-proclaimed redneck from the boonies. I should have given him a southern accent.

"Cat got your tongue? Did you forget to tell me you were mute?" he questioned, his head tilting a bit to the side. "I'm not opposed, just didn't bring a tablet to write with, and Divinity, I really want to know what you're thinking."

"I'm pretty sure thinking what I am, where I am standing, might give me a one-way ticket to Hell," I breathed, and his crooked smile sent a rush of heat to the very essence of me.

Chapter Two

PRESENT DAY

"Hello, Ms. Anderson." An overly eager intern met me as I exited the secure area at Hartsfield Airport in Atlanta. The 8½" x 11" sheet of paper he held had the Elrod logo with my name on top of it. "The baggage claim for your flight is number five, and I have your Expanse parked on the first level."

"Do you have a name?" I questioned, hoping the kid would calm down as we made our way to baggage claim.

"Yes, sorry, I'm Aaron, Aaron Buckly."

"Okay, A-A-Ron," I joked, and he gave me a double take. The worry that flashed in his hazel-green eyes disappeared when he tucked his head a bit, just enough to see the golden light catching in the bits of hair left in his high and tight buzz cut. "Breathe."

"Sorry, I just—you're the highest executive I've dealt with so far."

"Most days I put my pants on one leg at a time," I assured him as the light above the baggage claim began flashing and the conveyer belt began to roll.

"What do you do other days?"

"Wear a skirt," I quipped.

"I'm not shaving my legs." His retort made me smirk. "Not after last time."

"That's a story I might need to know."

"Not without a fifth of something toxic and a bribe."

"I think we'll get along good, Aaron," I said with a surety I shouldn't have considering I didn't know if he was *an* intern or *my* intern. "Who are you assigned to?"

"Me? I'm passed around like a joint at a frat party."

"Not anymore." I pointed to the first of my bags, and he quickly realized I had more than a bathing suit in there as he heaved it off the belt.

"You know they have a place for you to live. You didn't need to bring your bricks."

"A girl is nothing without the correct accessories," I pointed out even though I was currently in yoga pants, a tank top, and hoodie. Honestly, I hadn't expected to be picked up. I knew I would be getting a car, just hadn't put together the logistics of it all. How unlike me. Then again, I'd spent half the night packing and the other half rereading old letters and laughing at my girlish innocence.

I pointed at the second piece of my luggage. Aaron

reached for it tentatively before hoisting it over the edge and setting it on the wheels. “Shoes?”

“Yes, all shoes.” A laugh rolled up my back and allowed me to settle into the silliness with this kid I was totally poaching. “Have you graduated, or is this your last semester?”

“Last one, I’m at Auburn, but the only class I have left beyond this internship is online.”

“So a ’Bama boy.”

“Well, us that go to Auburn may be from the state of Alabama, but ’Bama tends to be for the Tide, not the Tigers.”

“Got it.” I made a mental note of the life and times of the Southeastern Conference since the rivalries and loyalties were even stronger than the hate between Ohio and Michigan. Sure, the Big Ten had its own share of rivals, but the SEC had a rich history of external hatreds.

After making our way to the parking ramp, Aaron hefted the luggage into the back of the car, and I placed my smaller roller bag next to the two suitcases. The midsize SUV would be perfect to get me around the country roads as well as tool around the city. Just enough room for projects and safety, but not so big I needed my own glowing-wand guy to guide me into a parking spot.

“Are you coming with me?” I asked as I typed in the address for the building that Elrod had rented for the executives. “Or do I need to drop you somewhere?”

“They crammed four of us interns into a lower-level

apartment at the Cherokee Rose," he explained. "I was told to drive you to the building and make sure you're fully settled."

Part of me wanted to continue my first-class treatment and ride in the backseat. But that kinda shit only worked when I was in "don't fuck with me" pumps and a power suit perfectly cut to my curves. Right now my hair was tucked under a scarf I'd knotted in the front, which made sense when my braids were out, not in, but I hadn't had time to fully invest myself in dealing with them this morning. Thank goodness for scalp caps to tamp it all down. Honestly, they were getting heavy, and part of me wanted to stop at a salon, but I knew better. I had to do my research and probably wait weeks, if not months, for an appointment with a decent stylist.

Part of me was happy that Aaron was driving. Having survived previous trips to Atlanta thanks to drivers that knew the area, I hadn't actually attempted to maneuver the streets, half of which had *peach* in the name. Detroit traffic was one thing. Atlanta had me wondering if everyone in the city was trying out for NASCAR. The fucked-up part was we were still trying to get out of the parking ramp, and I was already clutching the door.

"Isn't Detroit a metro area?" he asked as he merged seamlessly into the I-75 traffic and headed out of town. "You seem a bit nervous."

"We have different worries when driving in Detroit," I said, holding in my breath even though the kid wasn't driving crazy. That was every other driver on the road.

"Plus, I probably should have driven. Or sat in the backseat playing Royal Blunders."

"Not one to jump in the front seat of roller coasters?" He laughed a bit, setting me at ease. "You should try it."

"I'm a planner. I don't really jump before measuring the distance."

"Never?" he asked. "Come on, everyone has a 'hold my beer' moment."

"Not as an adult," I confessed. "Okay, not as a kid either."

"Must be why you're a big boss at twenty-five. You never had to take six weeks off to heal a broken bone."

"I'm twenty-eight, but yeah, only had my wisdom teeth out so far. Everything else is original parts." I cut my eyes a bit to the man in the seat next to me. "And you? How many broken bones have you suffered?"

"Okay, so what happened was my dad played every sport growing up." He tilted his head a bit before correcting himself. "He played every real sport. Baseball, football, basketball, and even tossed shot put through high school."

Eyeing the trim man who might be hitting five-ten on a good day with the right pair of shoes, I could feel my face scrunching in confusion. While I could hold my tongue, my face spoke volumes most days.

"I get it. My dad stunted his gene pool with my mother." He held up his hand momentarily. "The swim coach tried to poach me, so did the soccer coach, but—"

"Real sports, got it."

"I drank milk, tried to eat healthy, even lifted weights. Still I found a way to break a bone every season. I almost made it all the way to the end of basketball season one time. Then, on a fast break, I tripped on my own feet and slid face-first into a wall."

He brought his thumb and index finger to the bridge of his nose and wiggled it a bit.

"I think it gives me character, but the track coach was pissed I couldn't run until the end of the season."

"You are a good athlete then?" I questioned. "Just a fragile one?"

"There isn't enough bubble wrap in Texas to protect me from me, let alone three-hundred-pound linebackers."

We both laughed.

"At some point my father conceded I couldn't even make it as a kicker because I'd probably kick my own foot by accident and fracture the dang thing."

"But you played all through high school?"

"Alabama, you gotta be an athlete or a beauty queen."

"Couldn't work the heels, huh?" I teased.

"No ma'am, not with what I had left of ankles."

"Your dad over your failure as an athlete?"

"Now that my sister, Cindy, just made All-Conference for volleyball, he's appeased."

"She going to play in college?" I asked.

"Oh, that was in college. She's out playing at the University of Minnesota."

"Dang, they are always in the finals for the Big Ten and the National Championship."

"Yeah, it hit him hard her not going to an SEC school, but after me, I guess he understood you can't always get what you want."

Somehow he'd calmed me down enough as we made our way out to what I guessed was our apartment building, the Cherokee Rose. Only this was a complex, and he was in the apartments. I, on the other hand, was going to be in a town house in the middle of a row of ten. A few familiar faces were currently outside in similar workout clothes to what I was wearing: Devin Malik, the chief architect; Leslie Quarter, the new VP of human resources; and Chris Palmer, the union rep that would be the shop steward once everything was operational.

"Please say I'm only fashionably late," I said as I stepped out of the SUV and Aaron passed me the keys to the vehicle as well as my town house, number 906.

The buildings were new construction for sure, or had been updated recently, by the looks of the tan and taupe siding with brick-colored accents on the trim and shutters. Each had three steps with a black iron railing. No garage to speak of, but they probably didn't spend half the year under thirty-two degrees.

"We just got back from different facilities around here, ironically," Leslie said, bouncing a bit on her toes as part of her cooldown. She'd actually interviewed me for my internship when I was in college. In her early forties, she was in fantastic shape. Anytime I went to the gym at the office, she was already there burning up her lunch hour on an elliptical or treadmill. "You should come with me on the trails around here. They're insane. Then again, it's January and nearly fifty degrees."

"A sign of the apocalypse in Detroit."

The group laughed as Aaron brought my bags to the door of my town house and I went up the three stairs to open the door to let him in.

"Honestly, I could probably go for another walk? You up for one, Divinity, or do you need to settle in?"

"Long flight, I probably should stretch my legs."

Nervous energy abounded in me as I took in the three other executives and couldn't help feeling as if I should be with Aaron as an intern. Both men had gray hair. While Devin's was just at his temples, Chris had a full head as well as a rounded belly.

"I've taken my ten thousand steps for the day, ladies," he said, tucking the pickleball racket under his arm. "And a half dozen falls. My ego can't handle you two outwalking me on a path if it hits a small incline."

"We still doing dinner?" Leslie asked, and he slapped at his belly proudly.

"Of course, we need to talk numbers."

He stepped into his home at 908, and Devin went to toss his pickleball racket into his place at 907, then tucked his key back in his pocket as he approached us.

"So are you nine or five?" I asked Leslie, assuming the company had us all in a row.

"Two actually," she said with a sigh. "But both Chris and I are going to have to figure out long-term housing soon anyway."

"Not sure I could move full-time."

"If you saw the salary package, you could," she stated. "Plus, you get more for less here without having to do major renovations."

"Guess I'll unpack after you show me the neighborhood," I reasoned, happy now that I'd gone for being the casual traveler and not the bougie one.

Being the youngest by decades should have made me self-conscious, but for some reason, Devin and Leslie appeared to have no issue with my age. Devin and I had spent months going through specifics as he worked on the building design on-site and I the implementation phase. I was glad he was next door because I knew we'd have late nights, and now wouldn't require video chats, trying to make sure his specs and mine aligned. At times architects' visions were too futuristic for the realities of the world. Having the need for a lower carbon rating for tax incentives had added a layer.

"Tomorrow it starts," Leslie groaned as we made our way back through the blacktopped path with the mix of birch and maple trees. Their leaves had fallen, but a few clung to the branches as the northerners made the Georgians, in multiple layers, narrow their eyes as they passed. Probably blessing our heart as they did. "At least you don't have to deal with going through interviews only to give them extended start dates. People need jobs now, not in three months."

"You aren't hiring and sending them to other plants to train?" I questioned as we finally made it back to the houses. I could feel an ache settling into my hips from trying to keep up with Leslie.

"I'm only allowed a few weeks for line staff, a month for management," she sighed. "It's not like Detroit, where generational learning has workers half trained by the time they fill out the application. There are mechanics, tradesmen, and the like, but I'm having to determine the relatable skills."

"Quit your griping," Devin teased. "You know what they say in the South when it comes to hiring people."

"No." Leslie narrowed her eyes, ready to be lambasted with idiocy from the master. "What do they say?"

"If they come in wearing shoes, hire them."

Her eyes closed as if she were praying for him to stop.

"If they're on the right foot, make 'em management."

The shell of the plant was in place in Bended Brooke, Georgia. Devin had been living down at the Cherokee Rose for three months already, but now it was time for me to put the nervous system in place and connect everything to the main organs. Every item I'd preordered based on spec was now housed beyond the construction gates in a series of metal railcars. The list of which had me going only slightly nutty with my tablet as I walked down the rows with the head electrician.

"Spools of cable should be in the next one," Mark said as he used the master key to unlock the car and slide open the door. "I inspected every car personally when it came in. I know you said we'll have more coming in over the next few weeks."

"Yes," I replied, adjusting my sunglasses a bit to allow me to see the landscape of the construction going on, including the crane still being operated as they worked on the office space that would change the skyline of Bended Brooke. Hell, it would create one, since this was going to be the hub now for the South East District. "Hopefully before Devin needs to do the final install of the ceilings on the west side. Some of the equipment is easier to lower in than roll."

"I wouldn't know." Mark adjusted the yellow safety hat all those who worked with electricity wore on a construction site, an innovation Elrod Motors had adopted to make it easier on those looking for assistance. Plumbers had blue, construction orange, and management red. While I was management in a way, I wore yellow with a red stripe to indicate I was an overseer and more of an inspector than anything.

"Trust me, refitting for the modern technology? It's a pain," I said, remembering the partial shutdown that happened one summer. Allowing my parents more time with me had been nice even though I was at the age I wanted more autonomy. "That's why we're putting in the giant accordion doors to allow room for growth."

"Robots," he grumbled a bit. "There's no way we need to run this high of voltage for drills otherwise."

"Yes, there is a lot of automation, but there is also a lot of work for skilled laborers willing to learn new tools," I rebutted. "I have a pair of old wrench turners back home, and they appreciate that they'll be able to keep working longer with less strain on their body. If only they'd had this option decades ago, both of my parents might be able to go more than two days without Tylenol."

"Your parents worked the line?"

"They still do." I could feel the tingle that always accompanied my pride in my parents. It was corny and silly, but the fact they met working on the line only heightened my love of it all. "They finally moved up to shift leads and now are back to working the same time, but they know it and love it."

"And you build the factories?"

"Benefits of working for Elrod, scholarships for your kids," I said. "I know you're an outside contractor, but we'll need maintenance once everything is in place. I'm friends with the hiring manager if you decide we're a good fit."

"Are you trying to poach me on day one?" he questioned.

"You've been here longer than one day if you got this all organized," I replied. "I can't poach anything. I'll be going back home in a few months. That being said, let's have the fourteen gauge rolled out, and start on the east wing of the factory. Between the Peach Power lines and the solar being set up, you will be able to start testing by the end of the week."

"Solar? I haven't seen any solar around here."

"I was told the panels arrived two weeks ago."

"Right before Christmas?" He shook his head as he scratched at the side of his jaw. "I don't recall that at all."

"It was checked off in the inventory," I countered, irritation building. I thought he'd done such a good job I'd nudged him toward employment.

What was wrong with me? I'd joined Elrod with a ready-made team, and fear had me rushing to throw together one as efficient as the one I had back in Detroit. *Slow your ass down, Divinity.* I scolded myself as I tapped on the tablet to pull up the email confirmation I'd received.

"Right here," I said as I scanned the notification. "December twenty-first, you signed off on receipt."

"Impossible." Mark scratched at his chin. "I didn't work on the twenty-first. I took days off around Christmas since my daughter is heading off to basic next week. We had everyone invade my house for the holiday."

"Then how did I get this email saying it was signed off for?" I questioned, hearing the accusatory tone in my voice.

"I bet they had Ronald covering me. He's a journeyman of sorts we call in for day work."

"Ronald? And where can I find Ronald?"

"Probably at home."

"What's his number?" I pressed as I retrieved my cell phone. "I need to know why the solar wasn't assigned and where he put it."

"Oh, he won't answer today," Mark said with a slight shrug to his shoulders. "He only answers his phone every third day."

"Every third day?" My brow furrowed and eyes narrowed as I tried to catch the crazy Mark was tossing at me. "What do you mean he only answers every third day?"

"Ronald's a little touched," he explained.

"Touched? As in crazy? What do you mean every third day?"

"You know, three, six, nine," he said as if times tables were his go-to reason for living. "He only answers his phone on days divisible by three. I think it was his Catholic school upbringing. You know, the Father, Son, and Holy Ghost."

My mind spun trying to land on the wheel of autism where a person could answer a phone only on every third day—and more importantly, why this person was allowed to work with equipment with multiple layers of complex programming. Perhaps he was a savant in that area, but you can't put them in charge, and Mark was in charge here.

"Are you telling me I can't find out where my solar panels are for two days because it's the fourth?"

"He'll tell you. You just have to go to his house."

"You know that our company is one of the biggest in the world, right?"

"Doesn't mean spit to Ronald. Like I said, he's a bit touched."

While I wasn't for institutionalizing everyone, Devin's comment about shoes being on the right feet was hitting a bit too close to home. Sure, we could employ people with needs, but not being able to communicate by phone except on the High Holy Day divisible by three was another level of cuckoo.

"I need assembly of those panels to start," I bit. "Can I email?"

"Email is worse for him," Mark said, a bit of red flushing his cheeks. "Besides, it's an automatic process, and since he's using my sign-in...well, that's Ronald."

"Let me guess, every three months?"

"Pretty much." He cocked his head to the side in thought. "Which means he should have been able to send it to you, that being in December."

"Three is less a rule than a guideline for old Ronald then?" Irritation itched its way along my spine, and I knew soon my left eyelid would begin ticking if I didn't find a solution.

"You could drive out to his house," Mark suggested. "He's only over in Billingsworth, not more than a stone's throw from here."

The name brought a flood of memories, imagined ones, from when I envisioned the world described by Peter. I shouldn't leave the site, but Mark could handle getting the wires dealt with and laid while I go in search of the rogue Ronald. All the times I'd flown down here, I'd never made an excuse to go to Billingsworth. Damn Angela finding those letters. Peter had been out of sight for years now. Sadly, he'd never been out of mind. It wasn't as if I'd thought I'd seen him in passing or cyberstalked his name, but there were moments when people used a turn of phrase or I began warming while watching a sappy movie and remembered our brief time together.

Dear Divinity,

I've been the worst sort of friend. Your letter got misplaced by someone in the house, and I got in my feelings thinking you stopped writing me. I should have written anyway because so much has happened and you're kind of the best friend I have. Weird, I know, but talking to you is like how I'm supposed to be talking to God, according to my father. Is it wrong I feel less judged by you and so I can be myself? Part of me wants to spend twenty pages writing to you all about what I've been going through, but that would be horrible to drop everything on you.

If you can forgive me being a jerk and chalk it up to the fact I'm a pubescent teen (my mom's reason I am the way I am), *then write me back because you are dear to me, Divinity, and I miss my friend.*

Yours,
Peter

Ten Years Ago

"All these years you could have been coming up here and you chose stupid baseball," I grumbled as I lay back in Peter's arms.

His legs were on either side of me as we sat near the shoreline of the lake. Not on a beach, but where there was a tree with a bend like a seat Peter knew well. The beach was down around a curve about a hundred feet away. I could see where the counselors were building a bonfire over there and listening to what I assumed was Christian rock. The music was upbeat, but the words *Jesus* and *praise* were predominant enough they floated to where we were. We were hidden, yet totally visible if they weren't completely lost in the task and each other.

Peter's fingers glided up and down my bare arm, sending tendrils of electricity through my body. Even in the evening heat, gooseflesh erupted as the sun finally began setting. Summer days in Michigan lasted forever since the sun didn't go down until after ten at night. My parents liked to say the heat was what drove the kids crazy and started all the bad that happened, but they just didn't remember how many hours we had to get in trouble. Temperatures could be an irritant, but time was the real factor surrounding trouble.

"It does seem like a waste now," he said as his nose nuzzled along my neck, making my eyes flutter from the tickling and my nipples perk in a way I didn't know they could do when not below freezing. "How is it this feels as if we've been together for years?"

"We've known each other that long," I mused, the rush of hormones melting me into him as if we should be one.

Shouldn't I be nervous even thinking of giving myself to him? I'd never—well, I may have been the last virgin in my class outside of the AV club, honestly. I could say it was the nerd in me being a mathlete instead of an athlete, but all the others on my mathlete team had gotten some. Mostly from each other, but that didn't change the fact anytime I went on a date, at best they got a kiss and to hold my hand. And here I was in cutoff shorts and a cami, not wearing a bra, because Peter had already managed to talk me out of the T-shirt I'd been wearing over the cami. The bra thing was more because, technically, my camisole had a shelf bra, but I didn't exactly have the kind of chest that a strip of elastic could hold up. The extra-tight fabric was holding me in place more than the non-bracketed bra.

"I've known a lot of people for over a decade," he said. "Didn't mean their body fit mine."

"My body fits yours?" I laughed.

"Look at this." He reached down and wove the fingers of our right hands together, his on top of mine, and then curled them both to my chest. "I bet the other side fits just as well."

I turned my head slightly to where his rested on my shoulder, and our eyes locked. His, a sapphire blue, darkened a bit as I got lost in them. The mixture of pine, bug spray, and him lightened my brain as it rushed with the strongest drug known to man. My heart thundered in my chest, blocking out the music and laughter from the beach. Or was that his heart? I wasn't being held tight, and yet I could feel the pounding from his heart on my back. We were syncing up, our breaths, our heartbeats, our—his lips moved to mine, or mine to his? It was hard to track the momentum of the moment.

I got lost in the feel as his mouth opened and tongue teased mine to do the same. He tugged our linked hands, turning me as easy as one would spin a wheel. My legs parted as I straddled him, his hands coming to my hips while mine ran through his hair. When I tried opening my eyes, the world was a blur around me. No, not me, him. Peter was my one focal point with muted greens and browns surrounding him in a haze. The tree we were against no longer had definition in the bark. There was only the sensation building between my thighs.

The hardness pressing against the bundle of nerves

trapped behind layers of fabric had the center of me needing to be filled. Never, even in my own fantasies and exploring, had I ever wanted to be entered, let alone filled. I knew the logistics of tab A into slot B, but that didn't mean I couldn't feel a trembling inside me as if slot B were trying to grab on to tab A. My head was becoming muddled and overwhelmed, tossing me into surviving the base level of touch. Then again, the feels were amazing. Peter's hands glided along my spine, then cradled my head and tilted it back.

My lips burned, demanding more, but his had abandoned them, choosing to make their way down the column of my throat. The sky and ground flipped position. The rush in my head had to be from the fact he had turned my world upside down as his other hand began inching up and under my camisole. I was hanging with only his arm supporting my back as his lips created a trail to the crest of my breasts, and I had never known a more safe space. Even as a child, fear could grip me, but not with Peter. He had found a way of supporting me no other had. Physically, emotionally, and, if I let go fully, sexually.

I didn't even know where a rope to grasp on to might be. There was too much muddled between him and me, and all I wanted to be was laid out and explored. Was I actually floating at this point? I might have been. Even my knees didn't have the pressure pressing down on the ground. There was a shift happening, and now I understood his words. Our bodies fit. They moved and glided in unison. There wasn't the fumbling and miscues that happened with boys in my school. He knew me from words shared over the years.

Peter knew my dreams, and I knew his—the secrets, the good, the bad, the ugly. And even without ever touching my body, he knew it, knew how to guide and touch, how to shut down my mind running in a thousand directions. In his arms, I was his, and the world no longer mattered. Years of yearning should have had us tearing at our clothes and stumbling over each other's shoes as we kicked them off.

Instead, darkness crept in from the setting sun and the fact he'd moved both of us away from the lake. We were tucked just beyond the tree line where no one could see us, hidden, even though we were outside. I came up for air, not realizing I'd been holding my breath, and when I opened my eyes, he was above me, my back on the soft ground as his fingers danced on my skin. Kneeling between my legs, Peter flipped the top button of my shorts, then paused, his eyes burning into me with desire as if they could taste me as well as see.

"Divinity," he breathed.

I pushed up onto my elbows, the hesitation one I hadn't expected, not from him, the one who was so right for me. But fuck, we were at a Christian camp where everyone wore a purity ring. Was this where he asked for some weird thing to stay good with God?

"You wrote that you saw no sin in wanting to kiss my lips," I said, unsure of my own part in his fall from grace. I didn't want to disparage him, but an unfamiliar ache built inside me, one I knew would weigh on more than my mind if not sated.

"I want more than to kiss your lips." His eyes darkened, and in the moonlight, I caught a quick glimpse of his tongue catching between his teeth. "It's just I—"

"You what?" Cold washed over me as the music and noises from the beach started to leak in. "I know we're not exclusive since we weren't sure we'd ever meet each other."

"I always knew I'd come for you," he rebutted, leaning over and bringing his lips to mine. "I don't care if you've been with someone else. You're mine now."

Once again he claimed me with his lips, the weight of him enveloping me while his tongue explored my mouth and two fingers slipped inside my shorts and into me. The invasion created a sweet sting as I arched my back.

"I haven't," I gasped. "I wasn't saving myself, but no one has ever..."

Stars were appearing, but not from the velvet blanket of the night sky. They were from the rhythm Peter found between my wet folds, his fingers pushing deeper as his thumb began circling the bundle of nerves already throbbing from when I'd been rocking on him. This was happening, really happening. I thought it might. I also thought I might need to come up a few more times this summer before I got the nerve. Hell, two hours ago was the first time I'd heard his voice, and now his lips were moving down the center of my body as his hand began stripping away my shorts.

The lips that had scalded mine were now right above

the small tuft of hair I'd left just below my panties. He wasn't going to...was he? Guys didn't do that. They joked about it, but they never—a flood of heat burst up from between my legs when his mouth covered my sex, his tongue circling my bundle as his finger moved deeper inside me.

"Jesus," I moaned, only to be rewarded as he suckled the small nub between my folds. I thrust my fingers through his soft hair, grasping, as my legs locked around his neck as he continued to fuck me. He was fucking me with his fingers and tongue, and it wasn't enough. My want was turning into need as I cried out, "More, Peter, give me more."

He paused for a moment. The lapping and strokes halted, leaving me on the edge of what I could only assume was an orgasm.

"Please," I begged as the ache became a burning pain, clenching hard, and I released my legs. "Please, I need you."

He lifted his head, the wetness on his lips glistening, his sapphire blue eyes finally high enough to see over my breasts. We were panting, me from pain, him from a feral desire if his eyes were telling the truth.

"Don't call me Peter," he said as he climbed over my body like a panther ready to pounce.

"Wh-at...what should I...call you?" I breathed out in heavy pants as he hooked one of my legs around his waist and undid his zipper and buttons. He sheathed himself in a condom before putting the tip at my entrance and holding.

"I'm yours," he said, inching in slowly and gauging my

reaction. I pulled in slightly on my bottom lip, and once again he paused. The stretching of my core sent me over the edge when he placed two fingers over the bundle of nerves and rotated. "Call out *mine* when I slide inside you. Say it's mine. Give me what's mine."

"Give me what's mine," I said, the tremble gone from my voice. "Or I'll take it."

He plunged inside me, stretching me and sending me to another time, place, and existence. Any pain was quickly matched with pleasure as I clung to his back, not wanting him to slide out. Only he did, slowly, dragging with him any chance of me fighting the passion building to a crescendo. This couldn't be right. This wasn't how it was supposed to be. There was no fumbling or failing. He created a rhythm while burying his head in my hair and pressing his lips to my neck, finding a spot so erotic the fact I normally had it out for display seemed wrong, and yet so right, as he began to suck. The pinch of pain practically bruised, and I didn't care. I wanted him to mark me. Saying he was mine was nothing in comparison to how I was giving myself to him. Did he even understand how deep he was inside me? Not physically, but mentally. To me, he had been the reason I'd rush home and reread his letters over and over as I waited for the next. Delayed satisfaction burned into me at the end of a pen. Even now, the slow, steady pace had me clinging to him, and when his pace increased, I could hear angels singing.

Never would I have imagined losing my virginity in the middle of a forest with dirt and leaves underneath me. This was fairytale-worthy, and until Peter, I never saw myself as a princess. He'd taken my body to places I couldn't fathom, and when I lost all control, so did he, the two of us calling out into the night as if we were truly alone.

Present Day

Rolling into Billingsworth, it might as well have been my own neighborhood. Strange how the stories from letters had become all-consuming to me to the point I'd walked these streets in my dreams. There weren't many photos sent between the two of us. From time to time, Peter and I had mailed each other postcards, always tucking them into an envelope. It was our way of sharing a short note without our families knowing.

The image would be silly or sweet or show the beauty of where we were from: the sharp ice blocks that floated at the edge of the river, or sunset on the Detroit skyline. He'd send me aerial images of Billingsworth to show exactly how small it was, then some nature shots that made me daydream of walking through an orchard of blossoming peach trees just outside the town. Or finding a way to one of his baseball games, where I could sit in the bleachers with the rest of the town because there really wasn't any other entertainment without traveling toward Atlanta.

Hills dropped me into the valley where people had settled centuries ago. There were no blossoming trees kids riding their bikes. It was a school day, and outside of the remnants of holiday decorations, it could be Anytown, USA. But he'd been raised here. This was where Peter was molded and became who he was. This was where he'd been judged for committing a sin so egregious they'd sent him away. The sweet small town where churches ruled and the people followed.

Those weren't the stories in his letters, though. As we entered high school, he'd write to me of the parties where he had to watch the girls to make sure when they passed out drunk, they weren't violated. He spoke of the weddings he was in as a groomsman because "the kids couldn't wait to be bound in marriage for life" even though they had two years left of school. Really, the girl got knocked up, and the father wasn't going to let her shame him. It wasn't as if we didn't have pregnant students at my school. The parents just didn't force them to get married to save face, while others gave them up for adoption or aborted them before anyone knew they were even pregnant.

It was different here. The whole town could be in a Norman Rockwell Americana print, or at least the main street with its manicured lawns and flower boxes, front porches with only a set of chairs or a swing hanging, not littered with abandoned toys or even errant packages waiting on the homeowner to pull them in. A few houses had yard signs for students that were part of a basketball or wrestling team or cheer squad.

My GPS told me to turn left, and I followed down two blocks where the houses in need of fresh paint and a new roof were located. Instead of cars tucked away in garages, there were three or four along the curb or parked under carports. A few were even resting on deteriorated tires on the lawn.

Ronald's home had two cars, one of which had its hood up with a man tinkering underneath. The one in front of the house was a classic model from the Elrod line, a muscle car used in any decent movie where the main character was a gearhead, built in the late sixties, but without the years of rust it would have had if it lived up north and was out in January. This one was loved, but not in the way one would put it on a shelf and rev it up only when company was around. Slick black metal showed road dust, and the hubcaps didn't reflect the sunlight because they were standard, not chromed out. The gear-head in me may have gotten a bit warm in all the right places.

Walking up the short driveway, I could see legs in a set of coveralls poking out at the front of the disabled vehicle.

"Hello, I'm looking for Ronald," I called out, and the man under the hood smacked the top of his head into the metal.

"Fuck me," he snapped, placing his hand on the back of his head and turning his back to me.

"Are you Ronald?" I asked, and the man under the car

scooted out and extended a greasy hand before retracting it and wiping it off with a rag.

"That'd be me. The sinner over there is gonna have to repent for the foul language around a lady," Ronald said as he continued wiping his hand. "Apologies for my crude friend."

"It's all good. I'm out of Detroit. That's basically hello where I come from." I took in the slightly touched Ronald moving his massive body in a clumsy, but comfortable, way as he stood. He was at least six-seven, built like a linebacker, and had a five-o'clock shadow that might be two days past shaving. Dark brown eyes, with reddish-blond hair beginning to gray at the temples. Towering over me while standing, he slammed the hood down on the old Buick and sat on the edge of the hood.

"Now, how can I be of service?"

"Well, I'm—"

"Divinity Anderson," the man who'd disappeared toward the house said in a stunned southern drawl I had seared in my memories.

"Peter," I breathed, caught by a set of sapphire eyes that haunted me. My heart tripped over itself, unsure of how to beat as it pounded in my chest. Older now, Peter wore a ragged AC/DC T-shirt that didn't appear to be a replica. His jeans were stained a bit and dark. Worn-in work boots had him a few inches taller than the last time I'd seen him. My mouth became arid, and for all my daydreams over the years, this was not the meeting I'd expected.

Caught off guard and unsure of where or when I was,

years melted away while my mind tried to catch them before they were swept beyond my grasp. I needed them in place, the years of hurt and betrayal, but all my mind focused on were a few words of hope he'd put at the end of a letter. That he'd come for me, find me, no matter how long it took. That he'd fight his way back to me because he was and would be mine forever.

"That's—"

"The Divinity I talk about all the time." Peter interrupted Ronald. "Yeah, that's her. And I distinctly remember telling you not to call me Peter."

I stood, stunned, unable to move, talk, or even think beyond the moment evolving around me. Part of me thought Peter had passed away of an insect-borne illness in a remote village where medical care was out of reach. Or in a bus crash on a washed-out road. Worse yet, he was held for ransom, and the church didn't have the funds to bring him back. Angela was right when she slapped the remote from my hand anytime I wanted to watch a movie set in Central or South America. I'd needed a reason why he hadn't come for me or wrote.

In college I lost myself for a year in a mix of frat boys and fuck boys, the only difference being fuck boys didn't have the wherewithal to go through Rush Week. They were safe, noncommittal, and good for one night at best.

"Well, that may be so, but she's here to see me," Ronald boasted as if one-upping the man who'd disappeared from my life so long ago. "So, again, what can I do you for, ma'am?"

The poorly worded joke of a question wasn't enough to break my lock on Peter. How many nightmares had I woken from over the years where he'd died in the jungles of Central America, where he'd been sent on a mission trip after—the sharp inhale of breath I took made both men stare at me. I wasn't sure if it was the unwarranted attention or the memory of that night causing my face to burn.

"He's right. I was told you wouldn't answer me if I called today," I explained as to why I was showing up unannounced to his house.

"True," Ronald said. "The phone is a Devil's toy, and I do my best to avoid it. Have to say I'm impressed you made the effort, most don't."

"You checked in my solar panels," I blurted. "I'm sorry, I'm the electrical project manager at the Elrod plant being built in Bended Brooke."

"You make it sound like there's an Elrod plant being built somewhere else I might show up to work."

"Behave, Ronald," Peter warned. "I apologize—"

"For which thing?" I bit, the anger coming from out of nowhere. How had I been reliving the love I thought we'd shared, daydreaming about Peter, only to bite his head off the second I saw him? He owed me an apology. Even if he'd been sent off to the wilds of some other country to convert people to a religion they didn't want, he could have written me. Hell, I had his address memorized. My parents could have burned all of his letters, and I'd still know a letter sent to 734 Chambers Street, Billingsworth, Georgia, would get to him.

"If her eyes get any narrower, they might turn into lasers and cut you in half," Ronald said, and I shook my head, unconscious of the fact I'd been glaring at Peter. "Can they do that? I heard northern girls are different."

"They may be, Ronald, but I'm a woman."

"Yes, you are," Peter said slightly under his breath.

"And you signed for my solar panels, but didn't tell anyone or mark down where you stored them, and I don't know where they are. So instead of opening every container, I'm coming to the source to save myself a few days."

Crossing my arms to keep Peter or Ronald from seeing me tremble, I did my best to hide the fact I wanted to throttle Peter. But I also wanted to fall into his arms and be an utter fool in love with him all over again. I needed to leave, but heading back without the location of my panels would be stupid.

"I would have cross-referenced the containers I knew about and checked the ones I didn't," Ronald suggested.

"Or, you could have marked down the ones where you left them," I stated. "Or better yet, called in the installers to begin the process instead of wasting weeks in a container."

"Not as much fun. Plus, I was just plugging a hole for a day. I didn't know beyond receiving deliveries what I was supposed to do."

"Well if you answered your phone more than every third day, like a normal person, you could keep a job longer than twenty-four hours," I rebutted, trying to grasp how this system worked and if I would really have to deal with employees like this. Weren't southerners hardworking people of the earth, or was that a Midwest trope?

"Who said I wanted one?" he countered. "I own my home—"

"Inherited," Peter said, and Ronald shrugged.

"No mortgage," he retorted. "My car runs most days."

"More than every third," Peter added and leaned a bit, as if he were going to take a step toward me, then rethought it.

"Plus, I can fix most anything with a motherboard or an oil pan."

"Just not in the same vehicle," I said, pointing to the other sixties classic that at best had power seats.

"I don't like mixing things," he said. "You should see how many dishes I have to use to make sure my food doesn't touch."

"Or the plate would explode?" I shouldn't have been making fun of the autistic traits Ronald displayed, but what in the hell was going on, and why did it have to affect my part of the build?

"So you get it," he said.

"Not really, because they make plates with partitions now."

"She's got a point. Modern problems require modern solutions."

I didn't want Peter sticking up for me. I wanted to pull him aside and yell at him, tell him he'd crushed me for not fighting back or even reaching out. It was as if he was ashamed of what we'd done, when the night was my most cherished memory.

"Says the man still driving a Mamba."

The Mamba was Peter's? *Fuck me sideways, I'm so screwed.* It had been a favorite of mine because my father had one in our garage, cherry red, and his was a trophy one. I'd wanted to drive that bad boy all my life. The closest I got were my senior pictures, when he let me take some with the muscle car. One of which I knew I mailed to Peter.

Chapter Three

"Divinity," Peter called out after Ronald finally broke down in his grid-like mind to tell me where he had the panels unloaded.

"I need to get back," I said, wrapping my hand around the handle of my SUV and causing the doors to unlock.

"Divinity, please, you know why you came here, and it wasn't about work." He spun me around and pressed my back to the door. "You gonna lie to me? Of all people? We tell each other everything."

"Told," I corrected, my hands fisting at my sides and head turning away because I couldn't face him. I couldn't look in the blue pools and have him drag me under. There was no swimming there, only drowning in the mix of words and touches, both of which sent me over the edge. I was already weakened by having reread those stupid letters. I'd opened the door and let him in after I'd changed the key years ago. "We told each other everything, and you stopped. You cut me off with a shitty letter saying you'd try. Well you didn't try, did you, Peter?"

"I told you not to call me that."

"You told me a lot of things," I growled, my eyes narrowing again as he came into sharp focus. "But I care for what's mine, and you proved to me that was never you."

Cupping the back of my head, he leaned down and captured my lips in a move I should have remembered. One where I fell apart around him and forgot who the fuck I was. Who I'd become. Partially because of him. The taste of cinnamon gum mixed with my hormones and lack of being touched, causing me to grip his T-shirt, holding on for dear life, and once again I was safe. Two seconds, maybe less, and Peter had trapped me to my car. Our history threatened to do a system reboot to factory standards and me back to eighteen and stupid.

His skilled tongue tripped and teased into my mouth. No, I couldn't allow this to happen. I came to Billingsworth to find Ronald, not Peter. The fact the town was so damn small of course I'd run into him aside, this was not about rekindling a fire threatening to blaze between us.

"Stop," I gasped, coming up for air and pushing him back even with my fingers curled tightly into his T-shirt. My arms were extended fully, but a simple bend of my elbow, and he would be crushed to me once again. "I can't. I need to get back to work."

"Give me your number," he practically demanded.

"No," I snapped. "We don't do phone calls, remember?"

His eyes cut down to where my fisted hands were holding him at bay. "You're right, Divinity, as usual. I knew how to reach you, and I didn't. I didn't for all the wrong reasons."

"Because you got what you wanted and then got caught."

"No," he said, taking a step back, causing me to release his shirt, now a bit disheveled where I'd clung to it as if my life depended on it.

Maybe it did. Lord knows there was little chance of me coming out on the other side healthy if I started up with him. I was here for three months, nothing more, and it took us eight years to get together the first time. Right now my legs were weak, and I was glad my car was there to hold me up.

"I didn't get what I wanted." He shook his head. "My punishment was more severe than the crime."

"Crime." My head nodded up and down as a proverbial knife sliced through my heart and to my belly. "I've got to go. My project is now weeks behind because of your best friend over there."

"Ronald?" Peter questioned. "He's a good guy, just a little—"

"Touched, I know. I was warned."

"People that haven't seen the world use that term."

"Wow, I almost forgot you've been places and actually learned about people instead of indoctrinating them into a belief system you didn't believe in." The snarl coming from deep inside me spewed at him with venomous spines.

"I was sent away, Divinity," he countered, "forced to do construction and serve food to people who were hungry, but they knew better than to pass me a book and tell me to preach."

"And you just came back this week?" I accused with a shrug. "You're getting your bearings and were going to come for me finally?"

"I thought you were over me," he bit. "The second I was stateside, I switched my connecting flight to Detroit."

A chill ran through me as Angela's disembodied voice screamed, *"Liar!"*

"Went to the bus station and bought a ticket to Dearborn because all you ever talked about was going to the University of Michigan for college."

"And you went and knocked on every dorm room door? Hit up a football game and went row by row looking for me?" Flashes of me pausing because I swore I'd seen him came back to me. Angela had told me I was crazy and I needed new dick to forget about the old dick. Lack of experience had my daydreams being turned into wet dreams.

"I went to the registrar, and they wouldn't tell me anything beyond the fact you did attend college there," he said as I pulled in on my lips. "Much like today, it was chance I saw you."

"You saw me?" The words struggled as they pushed back the razor blades and lump in my throat. Freshman year I was focused, pushing through classes because I had been holding my breath for Peter to return. After that I had one year that was crazy and found myself empty at the end of it with a tanking GPA. I refocused, knuckled down, and finished strong. I allowed myself a boyfriend, all the while lying to myself that I wasn't settling, until the moment he asked me to marry him after graduation, and I once again fell apart.

"I did." He nodded. "Holding hands with a guy. You turned quickly, but the thing was, I saw him more than you —the way he was staring at you, totally dumbstruck and in love—and I couldn't face you. I'm a coward. I saw him and feared his eyes were simply reflecting the look you were giving him, the look that at one time had been my everything. If your heart now belonged to him, I'd see it in your eyes, and I was already destroyed."

"Destroyed," I scoffed, shaking my head, not wanting to believe him. "How do you know I'm not with him? That I'm not happily married with three kids?"

"The same way I knew in the woods I'd always be yours," he said, cupping my jaw and stroking his thumb along my cheek as he tilted my head up slightly. "The deep mahogany of your eyes calls to me, practically begging for me to come closer, wrapping me up in a gaze reserved for one and only one. And you, Divinity, would rather be alone than with a man who didn't evoke emotions strong enough to light that fire."

"You're confusing me, and I don't have time for this," I said when my phone rang in my pocket, pulling me from his trance. Retrieving it, I turned my back to him and composed myself before answering Mark's call. "This is Divinity. Did you open the container?"

"Yes," he replied, "and we're reviewing the specs. I've got my best men on it and will begin construction in the west field. I had the grounds crew go over the cleared area to trim down the grass. You almost back?"

"I haven't left Billingsworth. I had a few emails to answer, and I didn't want to do that while driving. I'll be taking off soon."

"Okay, boss, we should have a few of the posts in place by the time you get here then."

"Thanks, Mark, I'll be heading out soon." As I tucked my phone back in the pocket of my khakis, heat erupted along my spine as Peter pressed the front of him to my back, and once again I was trapped by my car. Butterfly flutters abounded along my neck when he whispered in my ear.

"Was there anyone?" he questioned. "Anyone after me?"

"Are you asking if I had lovers?"

"No, I'm asking if you were in love with anyone."

I wanted to say yes, deeply, unwaveringly, undeniably, but couldn't. The lie caught in my throat as his hand snaked around the front to my belly, untucking my polo enough to brush along my bare skin.

"Do you know how many times I stroked myself remembering the feel of your body? How tight I had to squeeze to replicate your sweet pussy? How I've been starving since the moment I dined between your legs?"

My knees became weak, and he pressed harder into me, the long shaft I'd assumed was standard, but now knew better, tempting me. An errant pinkie slipped past my waistband and stroked the quivering flesh of my belly.

"Tell me what I need to do, Divinity, to claim you as mine again?"

Leaving Billingsworth was harder than coming. On the way in, my hands had been shaking and belly tightening, but those eased as I found the familiar surroundings from Peter's descriptions. Now my mind was racing as I tried to compute all the new information laid at my feet. He'd come for me. He'd seen me. And I didn't need him to tell me which year because there could have been only one time when I was loved up with a guy. It was the year I brought the letters I'd lied and said I'd burned to my parents' home —out of sight and temptation for me to snag in the middle of the night to relive a vanquished dream.

As I made my way out of town, the Calvary Baptist Church marquee sign promised *A NEW YEAR AND NEW CHANCE FOR REDEMPTION FOR YOUR PAST. PASTOR PETER YOUNG.* His parents had won. The prodigal son had returned and now preached under the roof he'd felt too constraining as a kid. Redemption for the past, huh? Part of me wanted to show up on Sunday to hear if he was the same as his father, calling out even the littlest desire as the Devil at play. What would his parishioners think of him having me pinned to my car not even five minutes ago?

A mental note was taken for the time of service, but right now I had to get back to work, back to reality, and leave the childish fantasies I'd discarded away. The best way to do that had me pressing the talk button on my steering wheel.

"Call Angela," I commanded when the system beeped.

"Call Angela, is that correct?" the computerized woman asked, and I pressed the connect button.

"I'm hurt, crushed, and confused," Angela answered the phone in full-on diva style. "In fact, I'm pretty sure someone didn't even send me so much as a text saying she'd arrived last night. So unless you're a kidnapper demanding cash, I don't think I want to talk to you."

"I saw Peter." There was no reason for apologies. It wasn't like I'd been ignoring her texts since there were none.

"Shut the fuck up, you did not!" she exclaimed. "How? When? Where? The perfect Peter, the man with the perfect package, the man with the perfect lips? Is he fat, balding, living in a trailer with his methed-out wife and six kids? Please tell me his life is shit."

"Not sure his life is shit. I'm hoping there's no wife and six kids—"

"You didn't—did you? Divinity Joy Anderson, I know you didn't fuck the man in the first five minutes of seeing him. You did, didn't you? Jesus, is his dick covered in gold and hard all the time? Does his cum taste like Skittles? What is it about this man that robs your brain and pussy of all reasonable thought? Sure, he was hot, but now with his beer belly, balding ass, and missing seven teeth, the only way he should have stopped you was when his rotten-egg-smelling body odor gagged you."

I waited more than a beat for Angela to calm down, breathe possibly, and understand I wasn't about to talk over her. Not being in the same room, I couldn't put my hand over her mouth to slow down the barrage. I didn't know where I'd gone wrong: telling her how wonderful Peter was or telling her about the one night we had and the letter that followed. She'd never remember the good I had with him. For her, Peter had more red flags than an Ohio State game.

"Vin? Vin? Divinity, are you still there?"

"Oh, I'm allowed to talk now?"

"Bitch, you're not allowed, you're commanded to," she snapped. "Tell me you didn't fuck him."

"I didn't fuck him."

"But did you really and you're only saying that because I said to? Because I wasn't convinced with how you said that."

"I didn't fuck him," I repeated, knowing truth would set me free enough to get to the issue at hand. "But he kissed me."

"You kissed a seven-tooth-having hillbilly?"

"Stop. He's not fat, bald, or toothless," I bit, feeling a

surge to defend him at all costs. "The only thing that changed is he's taller and has a little beard."

"A douche-boy beard, right?" Angela asked, talking about one of those lines around the jaw and lips with no fullness.

"No, a good one, on a hot guy who is a grown-up pastor, I guess."

"Pastor? The man spreading the word or his seed?"

"For the last time, I didn't fuck him," I sniped.

"You didn't, but did those women? Is he married?"

"I didn't check or ask, but the way he was talking to me, no, he's not married. In fact, he's very much single."

"Is he? Is he really? Because I don't buy it." Angela switched me to speakerphone. "You're saying he's a hot pastor in a small town. The women are throwing their sin slides at him left and right."

"Get off Ticker and listen to me."

Angela used the social media app to stay current, only she watched videos with people our age talking about crap we were interested in. Couldn't really stay current that way.

"He wanted my number, and I wouldn't give it to him."

"Did you give him your address?"

"No," I said, shifting a bit in my seat in a personal pat on the back and straightening my shoulders in response. "Are you done telling me I'm stupid?"

"What did you and old Preacher Boy do?"

"Talked, he may have kissed me."

“May have? *May have?* Divinity, you went on for an hour about how amazing his kisses were in high school. Now it’s *may have*?”

“Okay, he kissed me! And yes, it was as good if not better than when I was in high school, but Angela, he wants me.”

The words hung in the air like forgotten party decorations a week later. This was stupid. I was being stupid. I knew better and didn’t need Angela’s approval to walk away from Peter. He’d broken my heart. Fuck his excuse for staying away from me. He should have fought. He should have come at me while I was in Trevor’s arms and kissed me like he had in front of Ronald’s. I wouldn’t have hesitated. My life would be set, and my damn sin slide would be assigned to Pastor Young.

“Say something,” I blurted because the silence had me wanting another rant.

“You, me, nefarious intent.”

“I can’t leave. I just got here,” I stated.

“No, me, I’ll find a way down. You stay work obsessed like always for the next week and a half. I’m off next weekend. I’m coming down,” she warned, and I could hear her clicking away. “I’m texting Deena. She gets buddy passes all the time.”

“Angela...” I wanted to protest, but couldn’t. Two days in Georgia and I already wanted to go back to the safety of my downtown condo and no threat of a man in sight. “Thank you.”

“Not a problem. Now, as for seeing old Preach, is there

any reason you have to see him?" she asked, and I knew I'd made the excuse to come to Billingsworth and next time I was sending an intern. Next time? There was no next time. This was a fluke and one I'd exploited for curiosity's sake. If only my kitty didn't have to burn to teach me a lesson.

"There wasn't really a reason this time," I confessed. "There's no way I could explain the little-bit-touched employee they use to fill gaps in coverage here."

"You left your job in the middle of the day to pop in on a town?"

"No, of course not," I said, and I did my best to rationalize my decision to Angela, who wasn't about to buy my excuses.

Luckily, no one back on the site gave a shit I'd left. Perks of being at the top, I supposed.

"Oh good," Leslie said when I arrived at the trailer we were using on-site for offices, hers being in the back for privacy reasons, while my cubicle space was front and center minus the faux cube walls. "You're back. Everything running like a perfectly oiled machine?"

"Not really," I sighed. "How long have you been down here?"

"Only a few days before you," she said. "Why? HR issues already?"

"Sort of, but I think it was an outsourced company."

"Ah, those I don't control." She popped a pod into the coffee maker and put her travel mug underneath. "I really should save this until three o'clock, but I need a boost."

"Interviews that bad already?"

"Haven't had any, I've been calling and setting them up," she said, taking a sip, and I watched as the warmth washed over her. "Now I've got people coming in already this afternoon. I'm not sure that's a good thing."

"Why?"

"They're available, which makes me wonder why."

"Night shift? High unemployment? Isn't that part of the reason we're coming here?" I asked. "I remember reviewing the specs around the level of education, unemployment rates, tech school and training. This area is full of eligible candidates."

"Maybe." She shook her head, and I could tell this was more than her current objections.

"Are the candidates bad? Or is it something else?"

"I'm overwhelmed here a bit. I had to go out to our SharePoint to find standard documents usually stocked. Then I had to print them off, and I had to stop again to refill the printer."

It was all I could do to hold in my laughter at the horror of having to put paper in a printer. Then again, Leslie was in her mid-forties and had been in management for over twenty years.

"Outside of the federal minimum wage and OSHA posters, my office is empty. The first person I need is an assistant, and I'm afraid my frustration over the situation will have me hiring the wrong person out of desperation."

This time I did let out a little laugh, feeling better about my own rush to hire. "You miss your team."

While I'd been with the company for only a few years,

Leslie had been with them for decades. Like me, she was comfortable with the well-established 120-year-old company. We had the blueprint, but we weren't there at the beginning when they had to start. Spoiled, that's what we were. At least we were aware of our stupidity.

"Perhaps."

"I get it." I felt better about blurting out job opportunities. "I'm the same way. I'm ready to snag Aaron for myself, and this morning I was ready to poach Mark from the outsourced company because he knew where everything was."

"We've been planning this move for, what, a year now?"

"Close to two for me," I said, heading to my desk, which appeared clean, but only because I hadn't been there yet. No pens, no paper, no blueprints. Only a hookup for a laptop to hardwire me into the system. Across from what was my desk, a three-screen setup was in place for CAD, computer-aided drafting, as well as other larger projects. No matter how complete the blueprints, it seemed we'd have a hiccup when it came to building.

"Then why does it feel like day one at a new job?" she questioned. "I know the company benefits inside and out, the federal laws, and even learned the state of Georgia laws."

"But you can't find the White-Out, paper clips, and sugar for your coffee."

"Exactly. I'd suck at being an admin."

"What I'm hearing is you never worked your way up from the mail room."

"There's a room for mail?" she joked. At least I hoped it was a joke, because someone had to hire mail room people. "I spent twenty minutes trying to figure out how to put paper in the copier."

"Breathe." I laughed a bit. "I think it's just a southern thing making us all wonky. A sunny sky in January is acceptable, but the wind not cutting through your thick coat, scarf, and soul seems wrong, doesn't it? I'm wearing a long-sleeve polo without a coat and regular sneakers, not boots."

"It's like a bizzaro world," Leslie said as she joined in with my laughter.

"I had to drive out to Billingsworth because one of the hired journeymen only answers the phone every third day."

"I'm sorry, what?" she asked. "Every third day? Who only answers the phone every third day? That's a thing?"

"Yes ma'am," someone with a sweet southern accent said, and both of us turned to see a younger woman with fire-engine red hair pulled up into a twist. Two sets of locks, dyed jet black, were framing her face, and she tucked one side behind her right ear. "Sorry, I thought y'all heard me come in. I've got an interview with a Leslie."

"That would be me," Leslie said. "And you must be Harmony?"

"Yes ma'am. I'll be going now."

"I'm sorry, what?" The already confused and overburdened HR rep was now completely taken aback. "Why would you come in and then leave?"

"I know how women your age see me," she said with a shrug. "No reason to waste both of our time."

While Harmony wasn't sporting a dozen piercings, tattoos, and spiked jewelry—though I was sure those items lurked underneath—she was far from the quintessential southern belle. Still, she was presentable, light makeup, minimal jewelry, and her pantsuit was starched and on point.

"Did you just call me old?" Leslie asked, aghast at her comment.

"No, but people like me—"

"Like what? Harmony Drummond, right? Top five percent of her graduating class at Terry School of Business out of the University of Georgia. Yes, you're highly overqualified, but I see you're working toward an MBA. With our tuition reimbursement plan, of course you would look for a job where you could step in as the plant took off."

A man entered the trailer. This one had line staff written all over him. Jeans were clean, shirt was too, but he wasn't in a suit.

"Here I thought I was coming to interview for an assembly man job."

"You are," Leslie said, taking in the room with three women to his one male status. "You must be Colby."

"If I'm not, I'll have to explain why I have his underwear."

I had to tuck my head, having more than one assembly line staff crack a joke or six to me in similar fashion growing up. Knowing no history, I was once again ready to blurt out a job opportunity.

"Colby, you're my one o'clock, and Harmony, I had you down for one thirty." Leslie ushered them to where we had a table with coffee, tea, and a small fridge with a variety of drinks. "Can I get either of you something to drink?"

"Coffee," Colby said as Harmony pointed toward a bottle of water.

"If you need anything, Harmony, please ask Divinity." Leslie passed her a bottle of water and a folder with the basic benefits of the company.

Giving a slight wave, I powered on my laptop. I began to shift around the timeline, now weeks off, and tried to find a way to reassign personnel to make up the lost days of construction.

"It could be worse, you know," Harmony said, catching me completely off guard because I'd been refiguring staffing assignments for over five minutes in silence.

"I'm sorry, what?" I replied absently, reaching toward my ear as if to turn off my headphones.

"Every third day, I know some people who only answer their phones every other day." Her fingers intertwined and twisted a bit as she nervously sat in one of the sterile office chairs provided, her feet tucked under and crossed at the ankle. "Which means they never answer, because no day is an other day. They think they're being cute, or that's what

I thought they were thinking, but my mama says they're a bit touched."

"If I had a nickel," I mused, absently twiddling and rolling a pen back and forth between my fingers like a mini baton.

"Well, you are in the South," she said. "Some do it because it makes 'em feel clever."

"And the others?" I asked. "You just let them roam free in society?"

"As long as they don't touch kids or harass dogs, I guess." She shrugged. "I'm from a little town about fifteen minutes from here."

"Wouldn't be Billingsworth, would it?" I queried as a frisson of electricity trailed up my spine.

"Yes, you've heard of it—wait, you're not talking about Ronald, are you?"

"You know him?"

"Of course I do. Then again, there aren't many people in town I don't know. Even with going to college, my family kept me up-to-date with all the births, deaths, and moves."

"My family did the same while I was in Dearborn," I said. "Only it was the happenings in the neighborhood."

Harmony smiled a bit, and I saw an opportunity. She couldn't be more than a few years younger than me, which meant she would have been in school with Peter.

"I actually had a pen pal from Billingsworth," I confessed as my stomach tightened, and I was about to back off from my comment.

"You're from Detroit?" Harmony closed her eyes for a moment as if trying to find hidden information. "What was that school?"

"SE Haskell Elementary. Most thought the SE was for Southeast, but it was for Sarah Elizabeth Haskell. Lizz was an activist with a plaque in the front. We all had to learn about her."

"Guess none of our pen pals told us about her," she said. "Who was yours?"

"Peter Young, not sure if you would know him."

"Saint Peter? There ain't a man, woman, or child in Billingsworth that doesn't know Saint Peter."

"Saint?" Was she really talking about the man who had pinned me to my car and whispered in my ear?

"I'm pretty sure he hasn't even read a dirty limerick in his life," she said. "Did he ever talk about anything besides God in his letters?"

"At first it was like that, but we kept our friendship going until senior year, actually."

"I wasn't trying to be disparaging," she confessed, holding her hand up a bit. "My family attends the Catholic church in town, but he came to speak after his mission in Guatemala and the second one he took in Honduras. Not really sure why our priest thought bringing in the pride and joy of Billingsworth would inspire us, but I'm not really the audience for anything religious."

Outside of believing I saw God the first time I had sex with Peter, there wasn't much about him making me think of him as religious.

"I did see a sign on a church saying he was the pastor."

"Not surprising, all the Youngs had it hard after their father got sick," she said. "I think he took over a few years ago. Were you able to see him? You said you went to Billingsworth today."

"Just in passing." I tamped down the building thrum between my legs. "You know, a quick hi."

"Saint Peter," she sighed. "I know girls that tried to break him over the years. He was in high school when I was in elementary, but girls talk and ignore little kids around them."

"Did anyone win?" I leaned forward a bit as if I were afraid I'd miss the answer.

"Not that I ever heard about. He should be a priest, not a pastor." She smirked. "Then again, there was a rumor about some long-distance love he met at a church event."

Chapter Four

Peter,

I've never gotten a love letter before, and I'm pretty sure I still haven't. But no, I don't have fifteen guys chasing me, I have twenty. If you believe that, I have some property on the east side of Detroit to sell you. That's only funny if you understand geography.

That being said, I wasn't raised with much religion. Don't let the name fool you. I was named after my grandmother's favorite dessert. At least that's the story I was told.

Divinity

Divinity,

Are you trying to throw me in the lake? I do know Michigan well enough. I spent a few summers there before baseball became life. Now, according to my father, it has snatched my soul, and I'm going to need a lot to be redeemed, but at the same time, he boasts about my ERA.

Peter

Hey Peter,

Not a sports girl, but my father is now questioning me since I asked what's so big about sports eras. Guess that's a different thing than when the Yankees were kings. Now I know you were making me deal with math. What did I tell you about that?

Divinity

Dear Divinity,

You told me math was your favorite subject and you were a few grades ahead of the rest of your class. Math is words to you now because it has letters somehow. Baseball is all about statistics. Does that get you hot?

Thinking I should be yours,
Peter

It was wrong to be prideful thinking girls were jealous of me, but I knew someone had to have broken Peter. No matter how much daydreaming and naughty talk we shared in letters, none of that could have prepared him for the way we were together. He was amazing, patient yet demanding, and the standard that all who followed failed to achieve. Over the years, Angela tried to set me straight, telling me I'd idolized him for lack of experience, had a severe case of Stockholm syndrome and brainwashing from a cult leader. She, unlike Harmony, was a fan of religion, but with limits.

I needed to compartmentalize. I had work to do, and running after Peter was not only nonproductive, but it wasn't who I was. And yet here I was, sitting at my desk, watching for Harmony to finish her interview, knowing full well I had to get my ass to work. I may have been in charge, but that didn't mean I didn't have to answer to people. Thankfully my phone began buzzing on my desk, and I answered quickly.

"This is Anderson," I said, answering Henry Witt, the head of my department, and my mentor in many ways.

"Hello, Divinity, can I get a status update?"

"Already?" I knew that was the worst thing I could have said and did my best to recover. "I was hoping for end of day. There was an issue I had to fix, and I was getting that together."

"What issue?"

"Nothing that should be concerning you. It's only one thing that can and has been easily addressed."

"I'm a sounding board, Vin. Don't be afraid to use me for problem-solving," he stated as if I hadn't found my own solution. "I'm who you can show weakness to. I'm not in charge of this project. I'm the one who said you can handle it."

"Just some logistics that I've straightened out, and I'm about to start cracking heads to get things back in alignment."

"Alright, but I'm going to be checking on you regularly," he warned.

Gathering my keys and tablet, I headed out of the trailer. "I'm heading out right now. I had to do a little work in the office to get things settled."

"Vin, I'll be watching your progress from here."

"Right now we're just trying to figure out where the printer paper is and how to get the coffee maker plugged in."

"Let me guess, you figured out the coffee," he joked with a slight chuckle. "You got this, kiddo."

Most days I had no issue with him calling me *kiddo*. There was a part of his mentorship that came from knowing him since I was a kid visiting the plant. I was transfixed by the spec designs hanging in the hallway from the early days of the company. He'd thought it was cute a girl was into cars—not realizing I was working the calculations from the angles, unsure they measured up correctly.

Today when he called me *kiddo*, it cut a bit. This was my first time out in the world truly on my own. I'd checked in with my parents when I got settled in the town house, showing them my new place on video chat, but I didn't have a safety net to catch me within the same metro area. I was making big-girl moves even though calling them that proved part of me was still a child.

Within two days I'd almost gotten us back on schedule. I wasn't popular, but I was here to get a job done. Harmony would be Leslie's assistant starting on Monday, but that wasn't what was front and center on my mind. It couldn't be. Henry was counting on me getting this project together, and the distraction had been enough to keep me from feeling the ghost of a kiss lingering on my lips.

My encounter with Peter hadn't been intentional, but the effect was as lasting as it had been when I was eighteen. I'd had an excuse to go to the place where he was raised, and I took it. Over the years, the man had first come to me in dreams, and the words from his letters came alive as if we had been face-to-face. Angela had tried to say the reason we never spoke on the phone was because he had a stutter or lisp or Tourette's and he could only be smooth in a letter. But there had been more to our interactions over the years. We poured ourselves into the words we shared in a way we couldn't otherwise. While most people could verbalize their thoughts and emotions, we were two souls united in the knowledge we were the keepers of each other's most intimate feelings.

I'd lost that part of me, and I no longer could put pen to paper. Journaling didn't work for me. I couldn't write to myself or even pretend to write to Peter. I needed to know a person I trusted beyond all others would take the happiness, pain, and confusion trapped inside me and protect it as well as share his own. Never could I have imagined when we were together, brief as it had been, that I could find the strength to pull the unspoken truths from inside me and admit them with my own voice. In the tranquil woods, even with the party going on not far away from us, the confessions we shared only deepened his hold on my heart.

"It's something, isn't it?" Mark said, shaking me from my thoughts and bringing me back to the harsh reality of the here and now.

"Wasn't sure we could do it," I stated as the whirr of bolt-tightening drills had the solar panel site breaking the silence of the meadow. Even in the middle of what should have been winter, green grass was still present. "Thank you for calling in extra journeymen to get this finished."

Part of me had expected Ronald to be one of them, but

my temper tantrum over the ridiculous exceptions made for the man probably had soured him, for this job at least. The budget overage had already been accounted for in the general fund, but now I knew I'd have to knuckle down to make sure all the other sections came in at or under budget since I'd used almost half of my allotted cushion. Sadly, that cushion should have been saved as a bonus at the end of the job, and if they'd done it right from the beginning, it would have been.

"Hey, we may take a minute to start our engines, but NASCAR came from the South. We know how to put the pedal to the metal when needed."

Mark and I walked along the completed section of steel skeletons, inspecting joining parts for security and testing the holds. Supporting less than a hundred pounds each, it was the tilting aspect as the panels moved with the sun to capture every bit of energy from it. Hinges were paramount to their construction, and the wires needed to control the angles had started being run. By next week, our generators would begin fueling from the winter rays.

"Ms. Anderson, ma'am." Jimmy, one of the local electricians, was hefting a bin with component parts as he passed. For the first time, I didn't balk at the *ma'am* salutation. The South had its charms, and no harm was meant—unlike the mocking around the word *ma'am* where I came from.

"You're doing a great job," I said with a smile. I was trying to find a bit of encouragement for my team. They'd be staying late, and I was going to stay around too, just back at the factory site. "I'm going back to the other site. I need to check a few spots. Then I'll be in the trailer."

"How late you staying, boss?" Mark asked.

"How late are you?" I countered, and he gave me a knowing nod.

The factory checks took over an hour, and I had to contort myself into positions that would scream for Tylenol by the end of my day. All of it felt worth it until I walked through a spot with plastic sheeting keeping the dust from moving to other areas. It wasn't the thicker vinyl, and the thin fabric brushing along my arm sent a shiver of remembrance of the light touch of Peter as his fingers trailed up and down my arm. Absently I brought my hand to my belly, the place where his thumb had slightly touched now nearly a week ago.

The man was more than in my heart and soul. He was in my skin, setting off frissons of electricity. Circuits I'd shut down years ago had been spliced back together, revitalizing the current. Only I feared more than lust sparking off, and if I allowed myself to fall too quickly, too hard, there was a chance I would end up burned down into a pile of ash.

Flickers of light from the first full connection being made when one of the workers threw the switch had the whole room brightening around me. The office space was no longer lit by portable lamps. Instead, the spot was coming together, and I could see the other side of what might be in front of me.

"And Divinity said, 'Let there be light,'" one of the

workers said, sending a chuckle through the men who were continuing to hang Sheetrock.

"Won't he do it," I said with a shake of my head.

Back at the trailer, I tossed my hard hat onto my desk and crashed to my chair as the day came to an end. Lifting my braids I had in a ponytail on the back of my neck, I waved my hand to cool the heat from the day. I couldn't wear shorts and a T-shirt on the site. The heavy steel-toed work boots that protected my feet had them practically numb. I knew I was stepping because I moved forward, but I hadn't been able to actually make the connection between the ground and my feet.

Bending over, I started to unlace my right boot when the door to the trailer opened. Leslie had been gone for a few hours since she kept with the regular nine to five. At least for this week, I was more shift based, which meant whoever came in was more than likely going to be sent back outside to review something. Retying my lace, I stifled a yawn the best I could before glancing up to see Peter standing by the door. He wore lighter-colored jeans and a button-down shirt with the top two buttons undone, his light beard at the same length as before, trimmed, maintained, and in need of tickling the inside of my thighs. I shook my head to clear the dirty thoughts as he broke the silence and brought me back to reality.

"The post office wouldn't forward your letter," he said, holding an envelope between his fingers with a yellow sticker on it.

"The post office isn't that fast." I eyed the ink-marked, yellowed envelope. "How long ago did you send that?"

"The postmark says about seven years ago."

"Makes sense." I leaned forward with my elbows on my knees. "My parents moved a few miles away to a place with a backyard, something about wanting grandkids to play there."

"You must have been with someone serious at the time," he said, a bit crestfallen.

"He asked for my hand. Sadly my parents said yes months before he got the nerve to ask me."

"And when he asked you?"

"Guess I wasn't as excited," I replied. Butterflies took flight in my middle as heat erupted on my cheeks. "My aunts and uncles were getting grandbabies like they were Oprah's Favorite Things. My mom was a little jealous."

"I hear that," he said, stepping further into the trailer. "I am the son of a preacher who believes in being fruitful and multiplying."

"Yet he only had one kid."

Peter tilted his head to the side as his eyes narrowed. "We had fosters. Didn't I write about them? I probably didn't. They were never there longer than a few weeks."

"Why?"

"We were the emergency fosters, keeping all that was needed for every age. My birth was a bit traumatic to my mother. They wanted more, but when they went to adopt, they found out about all the kids needing short-term care. Greater impact and all."

"That's nice." I was unsure of how to respond to the news.

"Yes, but my mother did mention the need for me to make up for her shortcomings. I could see the pain in her eyes as if she'd failed my father in some way."

The years of him writing about his father's judgment of him helped me understand the torment his mother had to have faced. If his child felt wanting, a person not from his seed had to have been crushed by his damnation.

"Why did you go back?" I questioned. "You were away. I'm sure you could have stayed that way."

"I could have. Guess I wanted to find a reason to leave and got stuck."

The awkward silence built between us. He glanced around the trailer, then walked over and placed the returned-to-sender letter on the desk next to me.

"Seven years, huh?" I said. "This was after you came to Dearborn, wasn't it?"

He nodded.

"Kiss good-bye or reasons why you were better off without me? Happy for me, sad for yourself?"

"I'm pleading the Fifth because I have no memory of what I wrote."

My fingers walked across the desk and dragged the letter back toward me. "That makes it intriguing to me." I wasn't about to divulge the fact I had been rereading his old letters. Having a new one, with untold love or disaster, had the envelope practically crying to be ripped open.

"Any chance you are done for the day?"

"There is." I reached down to pull the lace from my boot again. "I was about to go all Mr. Rogers and change my shoes."

"How about I help?" he offered, then kneeled before me, cupping the heel of my boot as he loosened my lace on my right foot.

"What are you doing?" I asked, though I wasn't sure how because I'd stopped breathing. The meticulous way his fingers moved had me petrified. "I've been in these boots for over twelve hours."

Fear washed over me as I tried to pull my foot back only to have Peter swiftly move his hand to catch my calf. He cradled the muscle, using it as leverage to rock my boot off and place it next to where my sneakers were.

"I'm not afraid of a woman who works hard." He placed the arch of my foot on his knee before running his thumb along the instep, bringing it back to life.

Tingling erupted across my foot as if it had been asleep. I moaned unconsciously, causing him to press deeper and find a nerve, nearly sending me over the edge. My leg thrummed as he worked circles on the sole before placing my sneaker on and tying it tight. When he repeated the action on the left foot, I lost all ability to think clearly.

"What were you planning for tonight?" he asked while double knotting my laces.

"Soaking in a tub for an hour while drinking Merlot and eating leftover Chinese food."

A smirk curled his upper lip as he went down on two knees, then ran his hands along my thighs, spreading them slightly.

"How big is your tub?"

"You don't have an off switch, do you?" I questioned, eyeing the man who should have been a stranger to me.

"With you?" He shook his head, pulling me up from the chair and thankfully holding on to me as I wobbled like a newborn foal learning their legs. "I'm pretty sure my off switch has been on long enough."

"A week ago I was the last thing on your mind," I challenged. I had to because the fact we'd been apart for over a decade and he was acting as if we were in a relationship wasn't going to fly. It was too fast, too crazy, and too much for me to accept.

"You're gonna lose your job at the carnival," he said, the sweet drawl driving me crazy and not helping with the weakness in my knees.

"What job?" I did my best to hold my composure. While I usually didn't play games, the logical part of my mind couldn't believe Peter had been pining for me for years. I was the one lost in a fairy tale, not him.

"The one where you're the guesser reading people's minds." Leaning down, he cupped my cheek and then moved in close to whisper in my ear. "Then again, I'm pretty sure you know what I'm thinking about right now."

Pressing into me, he moved me to the wall, and I could feel the swell trapped between us, hard, long, and making my mouth water as he brushed his lips along my neck. This wasn't the first time and wouldn't be the last this man would send my head into a tailspin. It was he who heard the door open first, the one who told me I needed to see who'd come in, and most importantly, the one who kept a hand on my waist to steady me as I moved to the side to see Mark standing hat in hand at the door.

"Sorry, Ms. Anderson," he said. "I...well...I needed a signature. It could have waited."

"No, it's fine," I replied, doing my best to cross over to him as he passed me the clipboard, afraid to step from the doorway. The last of the day's sun had set outside, and there was a blanket of darkness beyond the opening. "Anything else?"

"I'm assuming you want another shift on Saturday?"

I shook my head. "I think you've gotten us almost back on track. Tell your crew to rest up. It's overtime either way. We'll have a few more late nights next week."

"Yes ma'am." He took the clipboard after I'd signed off on the additional hours and men so he could push through his invoice. I saw him cut his eyes a bit to where Peter was standing, but when I glanced over my shoulder, he was standing with his back to us.

"School friend," I said, not about to explain the situation going on, especially when it didn't concern another employee. No HR violation for me.

"See you Monday."

"Yes," I replied, pulling the windbreaker I wore tighter around my body and zipping it up.

"You good, Divinity?" Peter asked.

"Yes, I'm fine. I'm not the little girl you knew."

"I see that, big boss lady. You done here?"

"Yes." I returned to my desk and retrieved my bag and keys. "Bath, wine, and Chinese food it is."

"Or," he said with a devilish grin, "how about I follow you home—"

"Stalker," I sniped, narrowing my eyes at him.

"If I am, I'm a bad one, telling you my plans."

"You follow me home, then what?"

"Then you get dressed for a night out and I show you a good old time."

"I thought that's why you asked how big my tub was." I actually bit my tongue that time. Who was this bad girl throwing lusty thoughts from my subconscious to my now stinging tongue?

"I'm not opposed, but I am a gentleman and was raised better than to proposition a woman into a compromising position." He raised his hands as if he were innocent when all I could think was the only reason his halo hadn't fallen off was because one of his horns had caught it.

"I've had a long day that was just an extension of an even longer week."

"Now I think you're the one trying to get me in the bathtub."

"No, but outside of putting on clean clothes and knocking off a layer of dirt, I'm not sure I'm up to too much of anything."

"I'll take it," he said, opening the door to the trailer and ushering me out.

"Why do I think you're up to something?" I asked as he reached for my car door when I unlocked it with my keys.

"Probably because you know me better than those who've known me from day one."

"As in everyone from Billingsworth?" I thought of my conversation with Harmony.

"Pretty much," he said with a wink. "Now don't be speeding. Some of us have warrants."

The headlights of his car stayed locked in my rearview as I followed the GPS, having not fully learned my way yet. Plus it let me stay engaged with the driver behind me more than I should have been. I nearly ran a red light because the glow of his stereo was casting darkening shadows, making his eyes hooded and jaw tight.

This was insane. Men who looked like him didn't fall for women like me. Even if I'd wooed him with words decades ago, neither of us was that person anymore. I couldn't squeeze into the shorts I used to wear without Spanx, Vaseline, and a minor miracle. Yet the look in his eyes was the same as it had been all those years ago, as if his prayers had been answered.

"I have never seen a girl as beautiful as you," he purred

into my ear as his fingers trailed along my arms. "I'd fallen in love with the girl in the pictures only to find out she doesn't hold a candle to the woman in front of me."

I'd never been called a woman, even at my birthday when everyone was talking about how I was legal and grown-up. They still called me a child and girl. Peter saw me as a woman, and damn if I didn't want him to make me one in the most important way.

This was crazy, I was crazy, and when I pulled into my spot in front of the town house, I was going to tell him to go. We weren't teenagers anymore. I had a job with responsibilities, and I couldn't stay up until two in the morning. Resolved, I was ready to open my door when he beat me to it and extended his hand to me.

"Thank you for waiting," he said, as though I were expecting my door to be opened instead of fighting with myself about what was happening around me.

"I wasn't waiting. I was building up the nerve to tell you to go," I confessed, and his head lowered a bit, catching me in the silvery blue of his irises beyond his lashes.

"Now why would you wanna do that, sweet Divinity?"

"Stop that," I snapped. "Stop being nice and gallant and—"

"Don't mix up your people, sweet Divinity," he warned, setting me back a bit. "The worst mistake I made was not fighting my father when he sent me away after the camp called about what happened. I should have run away. I should have refused to get on the plane, but I was scared. Trust me, I'm not scared anymore. I'm determined."

He closed the door to my car and stood over me as he once again pinned me to a hard steel object. Our breaths both quickened, and soon they were locked in unison. Pressed tight to him, I was sure our heartbeats even synced.

"I lost a decade with you, and then I tried to stay away, taking another week." Capturing my head in his hands, he leaned down, our noses brushing as his lips breathed on mine, but didn't make contact. "I refuse to lose you again for even a second."

"Then you'll have to pay," I said, finding resolve. "All you would have had to do to pull me from Trevor was to say my name from across the quad."

"Divinity," he whispered before planting a kiss on my lips, but I refused to let him claim me. Not yet. Not like this when my mind was a swirl of emotions. I wasn't fourteen being told by a cute boy that he was jealous he couldn't take me to our dance.

"I'm not eighteen anymore." I pulled away and headed toward my front door. "You have to learn who I am now, and you're not who you were."

He stood on the sidewalk in front of my steps and pulled in a hard breath before releasing it and sending me over again. "Basically, you're saying I have to fall in love with you all over again?"

I nodded.

"And I can't just fall for the memory of the feel of your body against mine? The fact I want to relearn the curve of your hip is basic animal attraction and not because I'm really in love with you?"

"This?" I motioned at my work clothes, meant more for a man than a woman with the blocky design. "This is basically all you've seen me in."

"Oh, I've been taking that off you in all sorts of lurid fantasies," he replied, taking a step up and resting his arm on the black metal railing. "But I know how to play like a good boy, as long as you understand I'm doing it for your pleasure, not mine."

Chapter Five

Staring at myself in the mirror, I couldn't believe I'd left Peter downstairs and showered. Not once had he called up the stairs to rush me. I'd shaved my legs, put on a cute skirt, then thought better of it and went for a pair of dress pants and a nice blouse. Fuchsia was a bold color and one Angela had insisted I put in my bag. The wrap design created a deep *V* between my breasts, and in another boost of boldness, I actually went sans bra. Tying the bow to the side, I let out a sigh before twisting my braids up into a bun and using them to create a column holding it together. With a swipe of a clear lip gloss and glitter making my lips shine as well as sparkle, I went downstairs to see Peter on his phone.

When he turned, he immediately excused himself, then hung up. "You're gonna need a coat, Northern Girl. Don't be telling me it isn't that cold out."

"This is practically shorts and T-shirt weather," I countered. "Almost melted today wearing jeans and a long-sleeve shirt."

"Nah, that's because it rained and sweet things melt when wet." The smirk that followed had me pulling in on my lips. "But you need at least a sweater."

Stubbornness was one of the leading factors that ended my relationship with Trevor. Him asking me to marry him was a foregone conclusion because I was supposed to do whatever he wanted, so there was no fear of rejection. He had the job lined up after college with a firm his father owned. My going to school was cute, but once we had kids, it wouldn't be necessary. I had been in a fog so long, becoming what he wanted and doing my best to follow what he said even when I didn't want to, it took Angela smacking me to get me back to rights. Since then, when suggestions felt like orders, I instantly rebelled, to the point it was second nature and I couldn't help myself.

"I'm fine. It's like sixty out even with the sun down."

"Alright," he conceded, not about to push, which, considering how much he'd been doing that lately, was almost jarring. "You gonna wear sandals or listen to me?"

My jaw twitched a bit, but I knew I should, at the bare minimum, choose peace in the moment and take his advice. "I'm assuming closed toe?"

"Yes ma'am."

"Okay, no, I'm called *ma'am* all day at work, and it's driving me crazy. Please give me a reprieve."

"And here I thought you liked being in charge."

Crossing my arms and narrowing my eyes at him, I waited for his contrition.

"I remember you had friends that called you Vin," he said.

"And I remember you didn't want to call me that, only Divinity."

"I'm older now, and I've changed. See? I've got things you don't know about me."

"So you're going to start calling me Vin then?"

"Nope, can't do it," he replied. "Divinity is a beautiful name. I'll stick to that until I come up with something better. Maybe as I get to know you better, we can find one we both like."

"Alright," I said, slipping on sensible but stylish boots with only a little heel.

I'd sat in Mambas before, loved the soft leather in contrast to the hard steel machine, and Peter's did not disappoint. The engine ran like new as he drove me not toward Atlanta, but out into the sticks with the radio tuned to the oldie country station.

"I'm sorry, I thought we were going to Atlanta," I stated.

"Did you?" He shrugged. "I'm pretty sure I told you I was going to take you out for a good ole time. That ain't happening in Atlanta. Atlanta is for—"

"Nefarious intent."

"That's a good way of putting it."

"It's an Angela and I thing. She's coming out this week and planning on taking me for a day of nefarious intent."

"Guess that's better than a night of it," he said as he turned down a dirt road, and every bad scary movie had me gripping the door.

Beyond the lack of infrastructure making the road pitch black with only his headlights leading the way, we had to add in the darkness of the pines on either side of the road stealing our ability to see. When he rolled up on an abandoned house and dilapidated barn, I pulled out my phone to see there were no bars. Only my heart wasn't racing from fear. I should have been afraid, and here I was comfortable because the car was warm and Peter was driving me.

"You good?" he asked as he parked, turned off the engine, but kept the power going, leaving us bathed in the light of his stereo.

"I shouldn't be."

"Huh, wonder why you are?"

"Because you're the best serial killer in the world."

"Well, you know what they say about us preacher's kids," he joked as he turned the stereo up and opened his door.

"No, I don't know."

"We're all a bit twisted in our own way." He got out and came around to my side of the car to open my door again. "Can I convince you to share a dance or two with me?"

"Is this how they woo women down here?"

"So I've heard," he said as a slow song began playing,

and he wrapped me up in his arms. "Not going to say I didn't try a time or three."

"Three, huh?"

"There ain't an innocent PK. Wish I could say there was."

"Tell me what happened, what really happened, the day after I came to see you?"

"Nothing much, a ticket was bought, and I was shipped home in disgrace."

"Peter," I bit, and he winced again. "What? I'm not calling you Mine. That was a stupid nickname. Want me to call you Saint? Or is that hitting too close to home?"

"Please don't call me that," he said, his fingers trailing up and down my spine as we swayed to a song about claiming the moment because tomorrow may not come.

I'd hit a nerve, one I hadn't been aiming for and one I would avoid in the future. The uncomfortable silence between us had been the first. Even in the car driving, there was nervous energy, but never unease. My stomach tightened a bit until he pulled me in closer and the heat from his body warmed me. Our bodies rocked on beat, and my head rested against his chest with only his yellowed fog lights illuminating where we danced. The smell of a cologne I couldn't place, but it was fresh, threatened to bring out my inner ho. Or that could have been the strength of his arms holding on to me as if he feared the alternative.

The song began to fade, and another rolled out with a faster rhythm. Peter released me, trailing his hands down my arms until he was holding my hands, and soon he was stepping back, then pulling me close, out again, and spinning me around so my back was to his front. Following his lead, we were doing a dance I'd seen in movies as a man sang about a watermelon crawl. It didn't take long until I figured out the pattern, and the smile on my face was broader than I ever knew it could be.

"Now come on, Motown, don't tell me you can't keep up," he joked when I stepped on his foot by accident.

"Hey, give me a mike, and I can backstep and spin in a line with my girls by my side."

"Okay, that I want to see." When the song ended, he went back to the car, abandoning me as he searched for another oldies station. He flipped his headlights to the regular white, bathing me in a spotlight.

"How did you find the Ronettes that fast?"

"What can I say, I've got a direct line to the big man," he said with a wink. "Now, show me those moves?"

"No," I laughed.

"Come on, Motown, you told me this was the real music. Show me how you dance."

Covering my face with my hands for a second to gather myself, I shook out my arms and caught up to where the classic sixties girl group was and put on a show. The moves were ones Angela and I would do when we found ourselves being silly at a sleepover—hip thrusts, spins, and trailing a hand down one arm. All the while Peter watched, his face glowing and not from his overhead light as he rested his arms on the top of his car door.

"You win. I could watch those moves all night long," he said, clapping it up and turning off the car. It took me a moment to get settled in the darkness.

Since it was winter, I couldn't hear the crickets he'd spoke of in his letters. Instead there was only the crunch of the frosted grass under his feet. He came to me and placed his hands on my hips, turning me so my ass made contact with his car hood, and lifted me. Unbalanced as I sat, my hands went back flat on the cold metal, sending a chill through my body. My feet dangled because I was afraid to rest them on the chrome of his bumper.

"The paint," I protested. He slid me back, and at first I thought he was going to spread my legs. Instead he moved me back on the hood and climbed over top of me before rolling to the side, and I realized we were both going to be sitting on the car. "Are you crazy?"

"I don't care about the paint. Relax, lay back, and take in the sky." His arm wrapped around me, and he pulled me in next to him. Above us was a clear sky darker than when we were in Michigan, the stars poking through the midnight ink, and we lay in the silence of the moonless night.

The cold was finally threatening my northern girl façade, but Peter brought me warmth as I tucked up next to him. We sat back in the natural silence only he could bring to me, the calm not bringing out my anxiety and need to move before it was destroyed by something worse than I could ever imagine.

"This should have been our Friday nights," he said, holding me tighter. "I'm sorry I'm rushing, but we missed more than years. We missed this."

"Trespassing?"

"No." A laugh rolled through him, but he didn't release me. "This was my uncle's place."

"Is this where you tell me how your family owned this land for centuries?"

"Nope, my uncle scraped and saved to get this place." The pride of ownership was clear in his voice.

"I remember you writing about an uncle you ran to when you needed a break."

"That would be him. He left me the place after the stroke. Told me to be better than him and find a good woman to make it a home, anyone can buy a house."

"This is your house? I thought this place was abandoned," I said, a bit embarrassed.

"I live in town still. My uncle had been having mini strokes for years. He called them spells," Peter explained. "With me being out of the country, well, by the time the big one hit, the place had started falling into disrepair."

"But that barn isn't a few years past needing a new roof."

"No, that's pretty much trash, but for some reason, he never wanted to tear it down. Should be the first thing, but it ends up being the last every time."

"How bad is the house?"

"You know in the South we get all of the deadly plagues: fire, famine, locusts—"

"Alabama fans," I teased.

"Exactly, one year here is like twenty everywhere else. Between tropical storms, flash freezes, and wood rats, any house is subject to disaster. Add a man who can't function, and doors get left open to the elements. Slow leaks turn into a small creek."

I nodded, snuggling in tighter because the cold was starting to bite.

"It needs work, and until earlier this week, I wasn't even thinking about the place."

"You're going to have me believe that you've resigned yourself to being a bachelor all because you saw me with a guy years ago?"

"That's my lie, and I'm sticking with it." A light laugh was followed by him rubbing up and down my arm, helping to bring heat to the coldest part of me at the moment. "Wouldn't you rather have it in your head that I couldn't live without you, so I withered away?"

"And you were content in the idea I was married with 2.3 kids?"

"You were happy," he said with a sincerity in his voice registering in a way I couldn't ignore. "Motown, couldn't you tell in my letters I wanted to be what brought you happiness? But I cheered when you found it on your own."

"And of course, now that you know I haven't, can we be realistic?" I said.

"I've been with others, but I didn't like it at all." The childish way he was acting had my lips curling.

“Like eating broccoli,” I replied. “You need the roughage.”

“See, Divinity, you get me.” He tapped my shoulder a few times, and I rolled on top of him, guided by him pulling.

His hands began sliding up and down my torso, each pass going further and further on my hips until he cupped my ass in his hands. My legs spread, straddling him, the guidance easy to follow with the reward pressing against my core.

“What is it about being outdoors with you that makes me want to get you naked?” he said while his fingers, underneath my blouse, splayed across my belly. Self-consciously I pulled in as if a flat stomach could ever be possible. “Stop it.”

“Stop what?” I questioned, balancing my hands on his chest, finding myself leaning down until my lips hovered above his.

“I know your body, every inch.”

“You know my eighteen-year-old body.”

“This one is better,” he said, his hands shifting to my thighs and squeezing. “You’ve grown into a stunning woman, Divinity Anderson.”

His lips found mine, and this time I couldn’t stop myself from being claimed. The soft velvet of his tongue danced seductively in my mouth as his hands roamed my body with the curiosity he had as a teenager, all of it proving he was far from a saint when he moved to where my bra should be and he found none. The moan was followed by a move I couldn't track. My legs locked around his waist as he slipped from the hood of the car. Our embrace deepened, instantly bonded the moment his lips met mine as he untied the bow of my blouse. With deft hands, he ran his palm over my shoulders before moving to cup my breast. His need to touch me seemed overwhelming as he carried me to the backseat of his muscle car and laid me out on the butter-soft leather.

Removing his shirt eliminated any fear I had over hurting him physically. His body was lean but muscular, with blondish-brown hair creating a trail below the waistband of his jeans. Biting my bottom lip only brought him crawling over me, licking from my belly to my right breast, where he suckled the hardening peak while kneading my left breast in his hand.

With his other hand, he worked through the final barriers, flipping the top button of both of our pants, but working mine down first. Screams from the worry about the leather were stifled in my head when he found my lips and slipped two fingers inside my damp folds. He stroked in and out while his hips pressed on the back of his hand. When he trailed and sucked along my neck, my arms wrapped around his head, and I fell back. Arching against his hand to have him go deeper, harder, and allowed myself to go over the edge, blocking out the outcome of the last time we lost ourselves in each other, the fallout that pulled him from me for what I'd believed was forever.

Knowing better, I'd lost all reason to stop him. I wanted him to take me in every way possible. I'd been punishing myself for his father's reaction and him losing his senior year with his friends. He'd found his way to me or I to him, the truth of it now bringing the only part of me I'd trusted as real sliding down my body and bringing my legs to his shoulders as he knelt just outside the car. His mouth found my wanting sex, and satisfied moans vibrated along my clit as he moved his suckling to the very essence of me, his arms locking around the thighs I had spent years trying to explain away for shame, gripping as if his life depended on their existence.

He drank me In, and I ground my pussy to his face, a rhythm between us increasing and a scream threatening to burst forth from the center of me. I floated. Real or imagined, emotions were washing over me from a hard week done, the man I had longed for, dreamed of, and not forgotten the feel of taking me over.

"Sweetest divinity I've ever tasted," he said when he came up for air only to increase his lapping and swirling around the tender bundle of nerves. The nub throbbed as he thrust his tongue inside me, then curled it, creating a deep vacuum around my tingling clit. When his fingers entered and curved up, I was done. The orgasm was a mix of pleasure, pain, and ecstasy exploding from the center of me. The blast had my back arching as I balanced on the crown of my head. Peter grasped me as if I were an unruly guest and he wasn't about to lose his seat at the table.

Every part of me tingling and tense, my knees were

suddenly at my chest, and his hard shaft had to push past the quivering, tight core. Three rocks of his hips had him so deep I feared organs being rearranged as I slid across the backseat and slammed into the other door.

"Fuck, you're tighter than I remembered," he breathed, my pleasure glistening on his lips.

"I...wasn't...coming...this...hard...last time." I gasped the best I could in hard gulps of air as my hands searched for purchase anywhere.

"Then it's on me," he said, pulling back slowly, drawing out the sensation on the tapped G-spot. "I'll make sure to never fail you again, sweet Divinity."

"Here I thought you'd started calling me Motown."

His mouth covered mine, the flavor of my climax present as a fresh peach at harvest time. "Now you know why I call you sweet."

Grasping my legs, I did my best to hold them back as he ground inside me. With one free hand, his thumb rubbed my clit as he began increasing his strokes in both speed and pressure, the hard pounding forcing me to grip my legs tighter. I wanted them wider for him, the angle perfect. When his sinewy muscles popped on his shoulders, I let go of my legs, and my hands slapped the cold window with condensation from the heat we'd created. I stared up at him right as he emptied himself inside me, not letting our eyes break their hold on each other.

His hard shaft pulsed inside me as he stayed buried, moving only his hips, his silver-blue eyes turning dark as he claimed more than my mouth this time. I'd fallen as easily as before. In his arms, the world was right. If only we hadn't been told it was wrong by those outside of the two of us. They didn't know what we had was more than lust. Our connection had been severed, but we knew how to repair it. Not him, not me, but us together could bring the two of us together finally.

Chapter Six

The sharp light of morning had me knowing I couldn't be a teenager. It was harsh and painful breaking through the glass of the Mamba's windshield, the frost from the temperature dropping overnight sending prisms when it found a crystal. It was the in-between rays shining through that hurt, stabbing me awake only to have me shift and be pinched by a knotted muscle.

"Fuck me," I groaned and tried to move before I got a charley horse.

"Don't have to ask me twice," Peter sleepily replied, pulling me tight with the blanket he'd put in the backseat and wrapped around us, before placing a chaste kiss on the crown of my head.

"I'm not really a country girl," I said, realizing I really needed to find a bathroom, "and I'm not really that kinky."

"That's a bold statement for seven in the morning."

"You said your uncle's home wasn't in good shape."

My bladder began screaming, and it was too close to a sweetly sore area, only confusing the nerves. "I really need to take care of a personal issue."

"Oh, well, you could use my house," he said, correcting my comment about it being his uncle's, "but I think you could be a country girl. There are trees everywhere. I do have tissue in the car."

"You're serious?" I wiped away the last of the condensation from the window to see the white frost on the ground.

"I'm not going to watch or judge. In fact, I'll go in another direction. It's at least ten minutes before a nasty gas station. We're alone."

"I've heard that before from you," I said as a shiver shot through me, partially from the memory and also from my stabbing need as I crossed my bare legs covered in only a blanket.

Peter scooted to the end of the car, opened the door, and retrieved his jeans from the ground. He shook them out and hopped up to put them on, giving me a nice image of his commando ass as he did. I watched as he walked barefoot toward the tree line, glancing over his shoulder before disappearing behind the pines.

Resigned to my fate, I snagged the tissue he'd left for me, wrapped the blanket tighter, and slipped his shoes on my feet. They were at least three sizes too big as I trotted in the other direction. Once relieved, I made my way back to the car, where once again Peter sat on the hood, this time the end of it with his feet resting on the bumper, his button-down shirt open as he took in the sunrise.

"You're the critter who took my shoes," he said with a smile that melted me as he waved me over. I curled into his arms and rested with my back to him. The blanket hanging off my shoulders gave him access to kiss my chilled skin, sending fire through my body.

"First you try to make me a country girl. Then you turn me into a critter."

His lips brushed along the nape of my neck, coming to whisper against my ear, "I wanted to show you who I am in hopes you'd fall in love with me."

"Sorry, I'm just in heavy lust," I lied, or maybe I didn't. What did I know of love beyond childish dreams and the feeling I couldn't find more comfort than when I was with him?

"It's a start," he replied. "I'll probably have to do the renovations to get you really going. You know a man with a hammer gets all the ladies crazy."

"That might not work. I'm surrounded with men wielding hand tools all day long, never won me over."

"Never?" he questioned. "Not once?"

"I think it's the connection with the man, not the task."

"Well, give me my shoes back," he said, scooping me up in his arms and tipping me back as I clung to his neck. "Drop 'em, Motown."

Kicking my feet, the shoes flew in two different directions, and I pulled in my lips to keep from laughing too hard.

"Oh, that's how it's going to be?" Peter flipped me over his shoulder like a potato sack.

How was he able to move me around like I was twenty pounds, not 220? With a slap on my ass, he walked across the field, putting on his shoes while I clung to him hoping to not fall. Then he unlocked the house and opened a box with steel-toed boots. After setting me down on the kitchen counter, he slid them on Cinderella style.

"Since you like wearing my shoes, I'll let you break in these new ones I got when I thought I was going to fix this place up," he explained, doing his best to tie them tight. Sure, I'd clomp, but shouldn't trip, and he lowered me off the counter.

The home had four bedrooms, two bathrooms, plus a powder room. He told me how he wanted to refinish the wood floors and attach a balcony to the main bedroom. The support system was there, but the old one had rotted out before his uncle took possession. Room colors, backsplash, and countertops had been thought out. The project would take years if he did it himself. From the falling barn, he had a few spots he thought he could reclaim the wood and use it for tables, in the kitchen for sure.

"You're going to need to update the wiring," I said, my attention drawn to the older fuse box so far out of code it should be criminal. "I'm surprised it hasn't burnt down already."

"The power has been disconnected for years. Glad you

warned me, or I'd be crazy and just call to have it turned on."

"You think you'll have enough free time with your ministry to actually get this all done?" I questioned, and his eyes narrowed at me. "I saw your name on a church when I was leaving the other day."

"Right, of course." He let out a sigh before a knock at the door made us both jump.

"Hello, county sheriff here," a male voice called out, and Peter headed toward the door, leaving me alone in what would be a kitchen.

For the most part, the house had been cleared out. The way Peter spoke of it the night before, I'd thought it was a hoarder's dump, but outside of dust, peeling linoleum, and a few yellowing pictures still on the wall, the place was clean. One of the pictures was of Peter as a little boy holding up a fish. It must have been a few years before we started writing each other, but I knew that little boy. I'd watched him grow up and he me. The handful of pictures we'd shared were the reason I never saw him as a stranger.

The sound of creaking wood made me turn, and Peter stood at the edge of the room. His face turned from somber to smiling once our eyes met.

"You beat the wrap?" I teased.

"What?"

"The sheriff?"

"Oh, that," he replied. "You'd think the neighbors wouldn't have anything better to do than call the cops."

"The neighbors? They saw us?" A chill tore through

me at a post-traumatic fear brought on by our shared history.

"My car, nothing more." He put his hands on my upper arms and rubbed up and down. Kissing my forehead, he whispered, "She saw an open door and car. Thought kids were being naughty. Well, she was half right."

"Not funny," I said as he continued distracting me by kissing along my neck. "We're grown, you know."

"I do," he purred, then nipped my ear, sending a jolt south as I tried to fight the growing buzz floating through my body.

"We have homes, with beds and—"

"Leftover Chinese food," he joked, and my stomach rumbled a bit. "Man cannot live on good pussy alone. For you, I'd try."

"Then what would I live on?" My mouth ached a bit thinking about the feel of his shaft on my tongue. Part of me wanted to know right now, but we had the weekend, and it seemed he wanted to spend it with me.

"So many options, but what do you have for food at your house?" he questioned.

"I told you, leftovers."

"No real food?"

"I've been working fourteen-hour days since I landed. I barely had time to unpack when I got in because I needed to check in with the others. The few staples I preordered I've already run through. I think I have some packages in the foyer, but I hoped to get shopping done this weekend."

"In that case, we'll make a quick stop before I take you home," he said.

"Why not go to your place?"

"You don't have clothes there," he reasoned.

"And you have clothes at mine?"

"I can toss these jeans in the wash and I'm good. You deserve a bit more than a quick tumble dry."

"I could wear this at your house," I said, dropping the blanket from around me and leaving it in a pool by my feet.

Instant hunger filled Peter's eyes, turning them from sterling to sapphire blue. The way he took me in turned me on in a way I'd never experienced. His hand instantly cradled the back of my head as I was pressed against the wall, and his mouth covered mine, the moment a mix of giggles and lust as his hand gripped my thigh and wrapped it around his waist.

"You can wear this anytime at my house," he said, his breath halting. "I can't believe what I'm going to say, and know it goes against my core belief, Divinity."

"I've already been the cause of your spiritual downfall once," I teased.

"True, but I need you to get dressed."

Never had I seen a more pained expression from a man in my life as he lowered my thigh, then himself, to bring the blanket back around my shoulders. He crossed then uncrossed the blanket for one last look before tightening it around my chest.

"After today, if I ever tell you to put clothes on, know I'm signaling that I'm in trouble. Or I have a brain injury."

"You better stop, or I might think you want me," I purred, tromping through the house in his boots like a child playing dress-up, though the mix of work boots and microfleece blanket wasn't exactly a character I'd ever seen before.

Dressing in a car was meant for the young. Thankfully we were once again alone beyond the pines, and Peter used the blanket as a shield. Between the fabric and the car, I was able to get back to my pre-debauchery state. Instead of a big store, Peter popped into a country market right before leaving the Billingsworth area. It was in what I considered the middle of nowhere, but quite a few people came and went before he made his way back to his car with two bags full.

While I took a shower, he tossed his jeans with darkened knees from the mud and dirt beside his car in the wash. I had some other clothes in need of a wash soon, so like we had done, they fell together, and Peter stood in my kitchen in a pair of boxer briefs and nothing else. He had found all the cooking tools I hadn't even considered looking for. Beyond coffee in the morning and a fork for whatever I'd snagged on the way home, I hadn't explored the place yet. The smell was all sorts of sinful from the sizzling round pork sausages, pancakes, eggs, and some yellowish-white mixture in a pot I couldn't place.

"Hey," I said, standing in my robe, bonnet, and slippers. Part of me was testing his response to a barefaced and basic me, the one he'd probably see more than the coiffed version. He couldn't have responded more perfectly.

Coming from around the center island in the kitchen, he placed a kiss on my lips, then locked his eyes on mine before saying, "This is the kind of morning I could get used to."

"Not really one I have experienced," I replied.

"Which part? The food or the backseat wake-up?"

"Either." I smiled, snagging a fork to cut off a piece of sausage.

"Can't wait for me to plate the food?"

"What can I say? I can't resist your meat." I chewed the warm, salty goodness, then lightly licked my lips, causing the sapphire to return to his eyes.

Peter,

Mine? Like a boyfriend? How would that work? It's not like we can go to the movies on Friday night.

Confused, but intrigued,
Divinity

Divinity,

I can't explain how it would work, but

I know who I want to be with would be my friend first. You are the only person I can really talk to, and that's the most important thing in a relationship.

Peter

Peter was right about one thing. If all we had was physical attraction, at best we'd have five years together. Okay, that was my now well-loved and pampered parts of me enjoying a man who wanted my pleasure more than his own. But our history led me to believe we could have a future. I'd imagined a strange confluence of us coming together because when we were younger, our likes and dislikes matched beautifully. Even the things we were opposite on, we soon found the beauty by the way we introduced the subject. Hell, I even looked good to the higher-ups when I could talk baseball in the Elrod suite at a Tigers game, all from him writing me about the physics, mathematics, and history of the game.

It was sad in many ways that his father wouldn't appreciate the passion he had for the game. Sadder still Peter had fallen for the pressures of taking over the church from his father. Maybe he'd been able to turn it into the type of place he wished his father could have made it, the one with the loving God, not the judgmental one. Lord knows I'd seen how harsh and black-and-white his father's rules were.

Ten Years Ago

The night had been magical, and I didn't want to leave. We'd broken more than the seal of meeting each other. I gave my innocence to him. I'd never be brave enough to ask if I was his first. It didn't matter, for he would always be mine. He held me as we stood by Angela's car as if letting go would be for longer than a few weeks. I knew I could make my way back up at the next break in the session, even if I had to hitchhike. Brushing my hair back, he tilted my head and lightly kissed my lips.

"You're mine, huh?" I said, trying to not grin like a Cheshire cat.

"I'm pretty sure I've always been," he replied, and my heart embarrassingly sped up to the point I had to tighten my hold around his waist and bury my head in his chest to cover the heat bursting in my cheeks. "Divinity, I never wanted to write that I loved you because I wanted you to hear the words from me first."

"Pete—"

"No matter what happens between us, know I love you."

"You're scaring me," I said, feeling a chill I shouldn't have considering the temperature.

"I don't mean to. It's just there is something I have to tell—"

"Young?" a man barked, and Peter shifted me to stand behind him. "That you, Young?"

"Yeah, Myers, what's up?"

"Whoever you have there needs to book it," he said. Even if I wanted to see who this interloper was, Peter had me locked in with his hands on my hips, keeping me shielded. "Keller's on a rampage, found some condoms in an area he was pretty sure he saw you."

"Saw me what?"

"Man, look, you know I think the whole purity ring deal is bullshit," he said. "But whoever you were—well, you know what you were doing, and I'm not going to say Keller saw everything, but he saw enough. I didn't even think you liked any of the counselors, but whoever it is will be publicly called out for sin."

"What if I don't believe anything I did tonight is a sin?" I said, finally moving from behind Peter to see a young black kid in a polo and chinos.

"That's between you and your God. We have to deal with the one in charge here, and you know what he's going to do. Your dad has already been called and is probably on the way."

"You should go." Peter turned to me, and I glanced

over my shoulder to see what had captured his eyes, pulling them away from me violently. Flashlights were cutting through the woods as if they were looking for a lost child, not following a sex trail of discarded condoms.

"This is crazy. What will happen to you?" I asked as fear crept between us.

"I thought we were far enough away, but I should have known. Keller is from my father's church and has been trying to get me caught up from the day I was signed up. Fucking deacon's son pushing to be pastor. Like I'm going to stop him?"

"You really should go," Myers warned as a bright light blinded me.

"Jezebel!" a girl called out.

Chapter Seven

PRESENT DAY

Peter was right. Once his jeans were clean, he was back to rights. I opted for my own pair with a light sweater and scarf. The ankle boots I had tucked into my bag last-minute pulled the outfit together nicely. My braids I wore down, and I knew I needed to either get them redone or taken out. The weight was an annoyance, and length was a danger when I was working. I hadn't planned on being this hands-on.

"I can't believe that was the first time you ate grits," Peter said as we made our way into the city.

"Why?"

"You know I have lived outside of my bubble, but everyone I grew up with ate grits." He shook his head. "Is it crazy I considered you part of my inner circle?"

"Kinda, half of what we talked about was our differences, though."

"Yeah, but breakfast doesn't count," he said. "Next thing you're going to tell me you never had biscuits and gravy."

"Okay, so, we had weird things in the North too."

"This is insane. Food is a staple. You're not in Costa Rica."

"Is that where you were sent?" I questioned, and the mood shifted in the car.

"Eventually, yes. Guatemala, Honduras, Belize, basically I did a tour of the Gulf of Mexico countries," he explained as his hand moved from my thigh back to the steering wheel. He was merging into traffic, but I was pretty sure the question was more of the issue.

"Eventually?" The word had too much weight when he said it for me to ignore the comment.

"I was sent to a boarding school for a few months." His voice sent a shiver through my body.

"I'm assuming it wasn't a *Facts of Life* style school, was it?"

"I'm pretty sure it wasn't even a school," he said. "The classes were online. It was the counseling where we had to discuss my sexual perversions that were a blessing and curse."

"How?" The word struggled past my lips as the words spat at me by the counselors at the Little Shepherd's Camp echoed from my memories. Those were a handful of minutes before I drove off into the night with Peter in my rearview being dragged from our spot in the woods.

"I got to think about you." He once again reached for my hand and brought it to his lips. "Hearing over and over how I'd defiled my body and shamed myself before God, I sort of zoned out after a while. It could have been worse."

Fear had me holding my tongue. Our night had been magical, and I'd fooled myself into believing he'd write and tell me when to come back. That I would be allowed to know where he was and he would claim me as his. Only no letter came. Instead I was left to stew and wonder, having Angela bouncing between it being a staged setup and him falling on a sword to protect me.

"There were people who'd been caught with same-sex partners," he said. "I was told if I married you within a week of being caught, I could be forgiven. My mama cried to me, sayin' I could have the girl I loved. That was when Uncle Jack came and pulled me from the cellar where my parents had me locked away in shame."

"I don't get why you came back here once you were free," I said, shaking my head.

"Penance. Not to my father, but because of my father. Someone needed to fight against the indoctrination."

"And you did it."

"Not even close," he sighed.

"Not that I would have said yes—well, I don't think I would have—but did you ever think about the alternative?"

"Marrying you?" he snorted. "Yeah, but there was no

way I could trap you in the life you would have had to live as my wife at that time. You wouldn't have been able to go to school or work, let alone wear the outfit from this morning—and I do want to see that on you often."

I smacked his shoulder.

"Damn, Motown, you offered first," he said. "But losing time with you was hard. I shouldn't have given up so easily. I'd been holding on for years in places I couldn't get away from, and seeing you was the straw crashing across more than my back."

His voice began cracking, and he swallowed hard. I squeezed his hand.

"Not now," I said. Heaviness weighed on my heart. "Unless you need to. I've always known you were taken from me and didn't go willingly."

"Did you now?"

"Well, mostly. There was a little bit of doubt, but I thought writing me for eight years just to take my virginity was playing a really long game and there had to be an easier way to get laid."

"I am a PK. Sometimes we have to think outside the box." His voice had lightened, taking a bit of pressure from my chest.

"That so? Well shit, I must have performed better last night since you sent the sheriff away…if he really was a sheriff and not your buddy Billy Bob."

"Had to have an escape plan in case you only partially rocked my world," he said as he pulled into a park. "No reason to waste my time with the girl of my dreams if it turns into a nightmare."

The place was packed, not that I was surprised. The sun was shining to fight the cold. Kids were on the playground, and runners made their way along the asphalt pathways. Along the edges of the parking lot, food trucks lined up with every variety, from soul food and poke bowls to tacos and burgers.

"You trust me?" he questioned as he brought me to one of the picnic tables set up in the grass.

Did he not understand the lighthearted question had weight to it? In this moment, for this instance only, sure, but in life? I couldn't say yes or no. Part of me wondered what he was holding back. It was right there, hanging out between the two of us, and yet I couldn't put my finger on it. The only way to get to the truth was to say yes, show him I was there for him, and then truly be there.

"Of course," I said, wanting to add "you're a man of God," but the only holy thing I'd seen Peter do was a few dozen heavenly orgasms.

My phone rang, and with Peter off on a hunt for food, I knew I'd have a few minutes. "Hey Angela."

"Girl, you would not believe the night I had," she blurted, no need for a "hello, how you doing" or anything more.

"Let me guess. You met the man of your dreams."

"Yes, but not the one you're thinking of," she said. "I picked up a shift at LoveJoys and ended up having to be the MC."

The shitty club was all about discovering new talent, but really they charged to get onstage even though no one was going show up at the place but scammers. Angela had been a part-time bartender since before it was legal for her to pour. It allowed her a place to showcase her talents as more than a singer. She was an actress, and if LoveJoys didn't bring out the improv, nothing would.

"And?"

"And, this agent from Atlanta happened to be there."

"And?"

"And I told him I was coming down this weekend, and he asked if I could put it off for a few weeks when he'll be back."

"You abandoned me..." My voice was singsongy since I wasn't about to be caught crooning in the park.

"Bitch please. Anyway, I hadn't bought my ticket yet. I will if I have to, but can you hold off for a few weeks? Will you survive?"

Peter was holding two Styrofoam containers between his hands, walking toward me.

"I think I'll survive," I said, not about to give her the lowdown on him just yet. While I shared about Peter, part of him was mine and mine alone, and I liked that fact.

"Promise? Promise you're not lying to me, because you know my broke ass was going to be stuck flying Cheer Airlines, and this guy will buy me Omega."

"Well in that case," I sighed as if really conceding. Peter sat down, and I covered my lips with a finger to shush him.

"I'll have to find my own fun for a few extra days without you."

"Don't work too hard. I know that's what you're probably doing right now, working," she said.

"Actually I'm partaking in the local cuisine."

"Are you eating Waffle House? That's not cuisine. That's a storm shelter."

Peter began kissing my neck and placed his hand between my thighs.

"Okay, my food's here, gotta go." Hanging up, I turned to him. "Sir."

"Ma'am," he countered.

"You're pushing it."

"Not yet I'm not," he said, sliding his hand further up my thigh to the juncture, "but I can if you call me Sir again."

"What did you bring me to eat?" I cut my eyes to the white containers on the table.

"Spoilsport," he grumbled, opening a container with ribs and greens, then a second with sweet potatoes. There was also a sealed one with something sticky pressing on the top. "Ribs, collards, sweet potatoes, and something I think you'll really like. I like it, forgot how much until recently."

"Then we should start there," I said, unsure, even between the two of us, I could eat all this food.

"Woman after my own heart." He popped open the dessert serving, and the smell of warmed brown sugar and peaches emanated in the bit of heat coming off the top.

Scooping up to have a piece with the crust as well as the

gooey peaches, he brought them to my lips. The cobbler was really good, with a crumble crust and a fresh peach flavor.

"The only thing sweeter," he said, whispering in my ear, his hand slipping up further and pressing my juncture, "is you. Do you remember when I kissed you? You didn't stop me even though I was covered with the very essence of you."

His hand began moving up and down underneath the table, and I kept my thighs tight together.

"Reminded me of a peach, warm and sweet with just a hint of sugar, only not from the fruit."

"We're not supposed to be doing the lust thing," I breathed. "Remember?"

"You know how fucking hot it was when you let me kiss you, tasting yourself? I almost came when you let my tongue in your mouth," he said as the rhythm between my legs began creating a fire. "Do you like the cobbler?"

"Yes," I said, trying not to gasp.

"Yes, what?" he asked, cupping my sex through my jeans.

"Yes, Sir."

"Never understood the term *good girl* until right now," he growled. "Fuck, we're gonna have to take this to go."

"No," I protested, getting his ass back by placing my hand over his hardened shaft. "You're gonna stop acting like a teenager fucking me every time the wind blows us together."

"Really?" he practically whimpered, his eyes downcast.

"Yes, plus there are kids playing over there."

"Good point." He removed his hand and shook it out, his eyes cutting down to my fingers still in place trailing along his shaft outside his pants. "Motown, if you don't stop molesting me in public, I'm going to have to call the authorities."

"What you won't do to see me in handcuffs," I said, pulling my hand back and reaching for a fork. "Sir."

There were times I questioned my choices. Then there were times when I shut myself down and lived in the moment. Sure, the second rarely happened, but when it had, I never regretted the occasion. Unpacking my belongings with Peter ended up being deeper than putting up pictures, organizing my to-be-read pile, and folding the last of my things. It brought about discussions that flowed and at times had us pausing to take in the time lost between us.

"Maybe I should pack up my house," he suggested with a laugh as he placed a picture of my family at my college graduation. "Then again, I'm wondering about the things you left behind now."

"Why? Because I packed so much random junk?"

"No," he said, picking up Sophia, my well-worn teddy bear, and sitting her up next to the throw pillow on the couch. "I like hearing the stories of your life, and the last box is almost empty." He flicked at her ear a bit. "I don't remember you saying you had a puppy."

"Sophia is a bear, fiercely loyal and vicious."

He leaned over and spoke directly to her. "I've been warned, Miss Sophia. But how did your ear become so damaged?"

I didn't need her most days, but I knew there would be a time when the old girl would be a comfort. Her eyes had been sewn on a few times and were a bit cattywampus now, and one ear was matted flat because it had been a woobie for me to suck on when I was younger.

"She had a rough life, being my protector and all."

"Here I thought that was Angela."

"Her too, only I wouldn't suck on her ear. Her scars aren't as prominent."

"Lucky bear," he smirked. "How long have you had her?"

"She was a baby shower gift, but my mom didn't let me have her unsupervised until after she was sure I wouldn't choke on her eyes," I explained the way my mother told the story, picking her up and placing her on my lap.

"Was she always Sophia?"

"No, she was Bear for quite a few years. Then she finally told me her name," I stated as if it were completely normal. My fingers fiddled with her ear out of habit.

"Sophia, if I were you, I'd be insulted she never told me about you," he said. "Trust me, I'd remember if she did, a bear of your quality."

"Why are you trying to start a fight?" I hugged her close

to my chest. "She knows my love for her has never wavered."

"Well, I know how it feels to be loved by Divinity," he said, reaching out and delicately taking a paw between his thumb and index finger. "You are a lucky bear."

He tugged lightly, and I got up from the chair where I'd been sitting and sat on the couch next to him. Like the night before, I lay against his chest with Sophia in my arms, and he turned on the TV to find an old movie. My mind wasn't paying attention to the actors. Instead I was imagining an evening when it wasn't Sophia, but a child in my arms. The way we shifted to stretch out and be with each other, my mind became quiet, even with the light brushes from his fingers and lips. This wasn't the hungry need for exploration. This was the touch of a lover in a moment of stillness.

My own hand reached for his, and I intertwined our fingers with mine on top and stroked the back of his hand with my thumb. Our day in the park had switched to a walk until we were numb from the cold and headed back to my place, talking about his travels and my handful of postgraduate adventures. We were learning about each other, even with our walls in place from hurt, our only true fear coming from being ripped apart for the second time.

I knew I wouldn't survive a second break. No matter how much I put up the front I was protecting myself, I wasn't. I was his, fully and completely. But we weren't children. My parents couldn't stop me from falling into this relationship, but I wasn't sure about his. He spoke only briefly about his father's battle with dementia and how his mother was in denial about the whole thing.

My eyes fluttered, and I realized I'd fallen asleep, Sophia in my arms, and a blanket had been pulled over me. The TV was on, but low enough it was more or less white noise. Peter was gone. There was a note on the table, scribbled out in the handwriting I'd know at thirty paces.

Dearest Divinity,

Thank you for letting me share a bit of my world with you. Maybe you should drag me up north for pierogies or pizza since you say your style is the real way. I had to go to work, and I wanted to wake you to say good-bye, but Sophia gave me the evil eye, and I knew better.

I don't need time to process what is between us, but there is something I need to discuss with you deeper. Know I am still the boy you fell in love with and who fell for you. My faith isn't great. It really is hard to be after how it has been wielded as a weapon for so many years. But there is one thing I know for a fact, and that is God brought you back to me because I've returned to the right path in life.

Yours always,

P.

P.S. Let's make texts our new postcards – 678-555-5673.

After I programmed his number, I folded the paper in half and looked at Sophia tucked in my arm. "You could have given us privacy. Don't look at me that way. It's different this time. We're grown. Ignore the fact I'm talking to a damn teddy bear."

I headed upstairs to my room and looked at the mess that was my hair. Pulling up my computer, I searched out salons, all of which were closed on Sunday, but I put in online requests to be put in the queue. Hopefully I could be squeezed in one night. Work was calling me, on top of needing to check in with my parents to avoid the cops being called since I hadn't contacted them.

"First week that busy?" my mother said as she answered the phone.

"Actually, yes," I replied. "It's a whole different world down here."

"You're staying strong, right? Don't let some bum Billy Bob try to run over you."

"Never. Plus, haven't met one Billy Bob yet."

"Give it time. How's your team?" she asked.

"Management team is good. I know I'll have to go to Devin's for dinner and review the sections we're working on this week."

"And the workers?" she questioned in her union rep

way. She and my father were both a hundred percent for the workers, but that didn't mean she wouldn't call them on their shit if need be. That came more after I was bumped to management.

"Fine, hardworking," I said truthfully. "Had a little delay, and with a few hours of overtime, we were able to make it up and get back on schedule."

"No chance of getting done early?"

"Oh, there's always a chance, but only if they triple my budget and I avoid a few labor laws."

"Fine, fine. I wanted you home by Easter, it's early this year, but it's all good."

For a family devoid of most religion, we did put a lot of importance on High Holy Days. It might have been about family more than actual celebration of resurrection or births. Something told me if I was in Georgia, I'd be seeing a whole lot of what Peter was really like around family. Only this year, for the first time, I was looking forward to Valentine's Day. I was seeing a future beyond my next project.

"We're really proud of you," she said, "just a little afraid you'll be wooed by the South. We know how much you always loved the area."

"It wasn't the area."

"Please, you looked at Georgia Tech for engineering."

"It's one of the top schools in the country, nothing more."

"Then why didn't you go when they offered?"

"Out-of-state tuition," I lied, knowing I'd been granted

a full ride based on my grades. I'd put in the application with all the others hoping Peter would write. "Besides, Michigan was my dream program."

Being a latchkey kid meant I had been able to keep Peter a secret. My father was happy I wasn't a big dater, and my mother thought I was too engrossed in my studies and needed to live. What neither understood was, I was fully invested in a relationship, more real than one right in front of my face. The few guys I'd dated after Trevor she refused to invest in because she saw the same look in my eyes she did when I was with him. Even Terrence, who had survived through the family holiday season last year, she simply called a friend. I tried correcting her only to have her tsk and say, *"Honey, there ain't no way that man is anything but a port in a storm. I'm not sure how you got your heart broken and I didn't see, but somewhere along the line, I know you did."*

I tucked Peter's latest letter in with the others as I finished talking with my mom, then dad. The hardest part of being down here was being away from them. How we had a close relationship had to be a reflection of their modeled behavior. My parents were loving and never faltered even though they were passing ships in the night for the most part. Days off were treasured moments, first with each other, then including me. They were practical parents who didn't expand their family, not because they didn't have enough love, but because they were already stretched thin and never wanted a child to question their devotion.

When my phone buzzed from Devin saying pizza had arrived, I grabbed my bag and headed next door. The weekend, while sweet, was over, and I had to be like my parents and focus on the task at hand before I could play again. There was no losing myself in a man, no matter how amazing he was. I'd worked too hard to slip up now over a crush come to life.

Chapter Eight

The week slipped by with memes and pictures being passed between Peter and me. I pulled my phone out as the image of a huge peach at the grocery store came through with a text asking, *Why is it I can't seem to get you out of my mind?*

To which I replied with a picture of a trash chute on the side of the building we used to avoid having to lug garbage up and down the steps, making sure my image appeared limp and lifeless. *No clue.*

By Wednesday he must have finished whatever he was working on. *Why can't I come over tonight?* he texted.

I'm working late and then have a management check-in dinner, I replied. *I'm a grown-up.*

Well why did you go and do that? he asked. *Like seriously.*

It's your fault my fairy tale fell apart.

The GIF he sent me had a man shot in the heart.

"Good news?" Mark asked, and I realized my smile was a bit too big.

"From back home, nothing here, sorry," I replied.

"We were hoping for a little more OT coming our way."

"I've spent the last three days shifting numbers to account for last week. That's an exception, not a rule," I said, feeling a bit of ire building inside me. Maybe it was because I'd spoken to my parents and knew how people made the job fit the time instead of the other way around. "Miscommunication patch, any slowdowns to get it again will be treated as that, and Elrod isn't one to reward laziness."

"My men been slackin'?" he asked.

"No, but I know what they are capable of when pushed."

"Or when paid a higher salary," he countered.

"I have room in my budget for bonuses. As long as we hit all the safety measures, I have no problem rewarding quality work."

Mark nodded. There was a simple way of dealing with workers: respect their craft and acknowledge what they do, all while letting them know they would be held to account.

My phone buzzed in my pocket. I retrieved it hoping to not be caught with more personal calls when working, only to feel a little deflated when it was Henry.

"This is Anderson," I answered and turned away from Mark.

"Overtime already?"

"Had to be done, big boss man. I weighed the options, and it didn't make sense to delay a power source. Solar went live on Friday. Saturday was bright, and when I checked the stores on Monday, we were already at seventeen percent. For winter months, we're already above projections."

"Were the projections done with Detroit's sunlight hours?" he questioned. "The weatherman says we get an extra two minutes of sunlight this week, but I'm not sure I feel it yet."

"I'm hurt, crushed even, you didn't consider my ability to adapt to new situations and consider all the contingencies."

"You insisted on thicker insulation for wires and pipes than what is recommended for the area."

"Climate change, old man, it's more than a talking point. The South is getting hit with storms, wildfires are burning up Canada, sending smoke to the North, and I'm pretty sure the Southwest has been turned into a crematorium. They just didn't get the memo."

"You're the one filling out the EPA paperwork, right?" he laughed in the rich, carefree way most in management couldn't pull off unless talking bottom lines and ways to cut costs.

"Not my job, but I've been consulted. I know you guys want to put that plaque up when we hit the carbon numbers," I said, not about to pull a full-on "I'm not doing it" speech, never with Henry.

"No more surprise overages," he warned, his tone shifting from what I was used to when it came to him.

"There something I should know?"

"You know I'm looking out for you at all times—and who isn't."

Unlike most big companies, Elrod's board stayed involved in major projects. Approving more than the budget, they approved every manager for every department. They wanted to send only their best, and "*a kid still flipping her tassel*" shouldn't be one of them. I was only five years post-grad and hadn't hit the master's program yet, but I was born and bred for this job, playing with electronics after school and doing math problems when others were doing free reading.

"Tucker?" I asked since he was the one questioning my readiness in the boardroom, or so I had been informed.

"Look, his daddy didn't put him in charge of anything until he was nearly forty," Henry said. "You can't help the fact he never had on-the-job training like you did."

"Thanks for the heads-up." I glanced over at Mark. Once again I'd jumped the gun. I didn't want the men to slow down, and now I had practically promised them the balance of the budget in a bonus by coming in under cost. "Any idea who my mole is? Or is it my progress reports?"

"Reports don't lie, but triple-check before posting them to the drive."

"Will do," I said.

After a few other instructions, I made my way back to the trailer, not defeated, just put in check a bit.

“Afternoon, Ms. Anderson,” Harmony greeted me from her tiny desk by the coffee station, where she sat with Aaron. He’d been MIA for the last week, and I’d missed the kid.

“Hey Harmony,” I replied. “You can call me Divinity when the men aren’t around.”

“I’m offended,” Aaron said, and I shook my head at him.

“You don’t count as a man.” I was digging the hole deeper for myself. “I meant the men working.”

“Stop while you’re ahead, Ms. Anderson.”

“Divinity, please,” I said. “They won’t let me steal you for my own, so you don’t have to be formal either.”

“Cool beans.” Harmony smiled broadly as she continued flipping through the new-employee handbook.

“Settling in okay?” I asked.

“Well, I’ve successfully not double-booked Ms. Quarter’s interviews yet.” Knocking a few times on her head, she continued, “Knock wood.”

“If you have any questions about those packets, let me know. I’ve been on both sides of the benefits discussion.”

“Okay. I’m on my parents’ plan for now, but I suppose I should grow up.”

“Please, between student loans and housing costs, use any discount you can,” Aaron said.

“Aaron, aren’t you staying in an Elrod apartment?”

“With three other interns,” he countered.

“Touché.”

A text came through, and I had to turn to not be caught blushing.

Friday night, wear my favorite outfit with heels.

We're dining in? I replied.

I am.

I shook my head at his bold flirtations.

I miss you, and yes, you can put on a dress with the heels before we come home, remove them after.

Home?

Divinity, wherever you are is my home.

Glancing up at Harmony, I could see she was working between the book and her computer. While I hated to bug her, a part of me wanted to know more about Peter. Sure, he was a little older than her, but the boy she'd briefly described didn't match the man shamelessly flirting with me at all hours.

"Um, Harmony?" I said, and her head popped up, the true red hair a shining greeting even the staunchest critic couldn't deny.

"Yes?"

"Saint Peter, the kid from your hometown, not the guy at the gate—"

"One and the same if you ask me," she replied, resting her chin on her upturned hand. "It's a good thing he's a preacher. If he became a judge, our jail cells would be bursting at the seams."

"Really? He's that big of a jerk?"

"I shouldn't say anything." Harmony waved her hand as if to clear the air.

"No, you should. See, the guy who wrote me letters didn't seem like the type to stand in judgment of people."

"Wait, am I missing dish?" Aaron asked. "I need to be in the know."

"Do you?" I mocked. "Or do you need to go somewhere?"

He ran an invisible zipper over his lips and winked in approval.

"Having a double life, that's how all those zealots are," she said. "Trust me, I grew up here. Baptists, Evangelicals, even the run-of-the-mill church lady would damn you to Hell for breathing wrong or jaywalking."

"What's the biggest sin?" I questioned.

"Depends on the church, but for Saint Peter, I'd say carnal desires." Her head bobbed up and down as if agreeing with her assessment. "Yep, makes you wonder if he's a secret Freddie Mercury fan. Any hint in your letters?"

"Not leaning that way," I said, thinking the man would be highly overcompensating if he was. Aaron smirked a bit, but stayed silent.

"Damn, that'll piss my sister off. She always had a thing for him," she sighed.

The door opened, and a girl practically blew in, tousling the short blue pixie cut she sported with one hand and holding a motorcycle helmet with the other. She gave Harmony a quick nod before turning toward me. Her neck tat went all the way to her chin and just below her hairline in the back. With pierced eyebrows, an oxen piercing in her nose, and mods at least an inch across in her ears, she made Harmony look like a Catholic schoolgirl.

"Hey, I've got a delivery for a Devin Malik," she said, pulling out a long round tube as I sat a bit dumbfounded. Elrod had courier service plans. Why would a random messenger be dropping off what could only be a set of blueprints? For that matter, why would he need one processed? All the plans were finalized. "Hello? You Devin?"

"Me?" I was about to be insulted until I thought about the fact Devin was both a male and female name. "No, I'm not, but I can sign for him."

"Cool." She took out a scanner to pull up the bill of lading. Crossing the room, she pointed the tube at me, but didn't hand it over. "I know you, don't I?"

"I highly doubt it. I've been in town less than a week," I said, reaching for the tube only to have her sharply pull it back.

"No, I know your face." She bounced the tube on her head as if it would loosen her thoughts. "I never forget a face. This is going to drive me crazy all night. What's your name?"

"I don't believe that's any of your business," I countered, a bit put off by the wild woman in ripped jeans and a leather jacket that zipped at an angle.

"It is if you want the package." As she waved her scanner at me, I could see the keyboard. She tucked the tube under her arm, both thumbs at the ready to type my name.

“Divinity Anderson,” I said.

“Not ringing any bells.” She shook her head before hitting enter and passing me the tube. Her hazel eyes met mine, and I suddenly felt self-conscious, as if judged. A flash of a memory hit us both at the same time. “Jezebel.”

“I know you did not just call me that.”

“I’m sorry, I remember you now from Little Shepherd’s. I was fucked up back then, drinking the Kool-Aid and all that. I can’t believe how righteous I thought I was when I found—” She took a step back and closed her eyes. “I cannot apologize enough for what I did to you.”

“Me? What about—”

“Oh, you don’t even need to say it. I’ve tried to apologize to him a thousand times, but I get it. Trust I ended up in a similar place because I was caught with prescription cough syrup.” This stranger who I wanted to stay that way dropped her head in shame. “If you see Young, tell him I really am sorry.”

“That’s not my favorite outfit,” Peter said when I opened the door wearing the red bottoms and the dress I needed a shoehorn to get into. “It is high on the list, though. Damn, woman, you’re a poster for sin.”

His eyes followed his hand that ran along the curve from my side to hip. He was smartly dressed, light brown dress shoes with navy slacks, a button-down, and gray sweater vest. But it was his beard I couldn't get enough of as I rubbed the light scruff I'd been missing on my palm.

"I wouldn't open the door in your favorite outfit," I said, turning my head to the side, allowing him to kiss along my neck. "I have coworkers all around me."

"You think you're being watched?"

"No," I stated plainly. "I know I am."

He took my hand in his and intertwined our fingers, bringing me to his car. Opening the door, he placed his hand on the roof at the top of it, a minor gesture, but one I noted. Once again he drove me into the city. Only this time we went to the top of a skyscraper for dinner, and he sat across from me and allowed the meal to come to us instead, using the food as a metaphor. Under the table my foot absently ran along his calf as he told me about how he had been getting all the measurements to deal with his uncle's home.

"I told you the first thing you needed to do was fix your fuse box. It needs to be upgraded to 220."

"When can you do that?"

"Sir," I said, the normally admonishing phrase coming out so differently when said to him. "Peter."

"No, keep with the Sir." He waved over the waiter to refill our wineglasses.

"I'm not a residential electrician."

"And yet," he pointed out, raising and tipping his glass to mine, "you diagnosed a problem."

“I can tell you a man’s choking, doesn’t mean I’m a doctor.”

“Come on, don’t you want to come over tomorrow and spend the day rewiring an old house?”

“Wow, stay home curled up with a good book or rewire a house?” My hands weighed the options, and he shook his head at me.

“How about I make it worth your while?”

“And how is that?” I asked just as he reached under the table, caught my ankle, and placed my foot in his lap under the tablecloth. After popping off my heel, he rubbed my foot, finding spots that sent a rush to other parts of my body. “Peter.”

“I don’t answer to that.”

“Sir, stop it.”

“Why?” he teased, pressing along my instep. “You seem to be enjoying it.”

“Any dessert for you two tonight?” our waiter questioning as he approached. “We have a baked Alaska on special. Then there is always our cheesecake, as well as an assortment of modernized cobblers.”

“Peach by chance?” Peter asked, and I instantly spoke up.

“We’d love the baked Alaska.” I wasn’t repeating the park, when the man had pushed my foot against his hardened shaft and locked me in with his thighs since he was leaning on the table.

The waiter looked to Peter as if what I’d said didn’t matter. Thankfully Peter gave him a nod of approval, and he went to put the order in. I'd been debating for two days if I should tell him about the delivery girl. All through dinner I could feel it eating at the back of my mind, and even right now, with him completely focused on me, I couldn't help feeling as if I were lying to him by not bringing it up.

"What's going on, Motown?" he said, reaching down to slide my shoe back onto my foot. "You keep nibbling on the inside of your cheek any more, there's a chance you'll make it all the way through."

My tongue went to the left side of my cheek to find he was right. I'd moved away from the edge of my bottom lip because people figured it out quickly. The fact I'd moved over to my cheek and he instantly caught it was soothing in a way. Never had anyone been fully attuned to me, and here he was focused and attentive.

"Remember the girl who yelled at me that night at Little Shepherd?"

His jaw ticked, and he glanced to the side, pulling in on his lips before settling back into focusing on me. "Yeah."

"She was doing a delivery at the jobsite the other day."

"How the mighty have fallen," he chortled, leaning back in his chair. "Or was it Gideon Bibles she was dropping off in hopes of saving your soul?"

"You haven't seen her?"

"Not in years. She's sent me emails, but I don't even open them. Trust me, there's nothing she could say I'd be interested in."

"She wanted to apologize," I said somberly.

"Too little too late." His eyes darkened, but not to the sapphire of lust. This was navy and harsh. "She acted all high-and-mighty, the purity I should have been wanting."

"Wait, did she turn you in because she was jealous?"

"I was one of two she wanted," he explained, "and she used turning me in to prove herself to the other guy. So, no, I'm not interested in her reasons."

"Well she must not be with him now," I said, remembering the tatted biker.

"No, she's not, but that doesn't change that she destroyed my life and took you from me." His hand slid across the table to mine. Once they clasped, he stroked across the top of my hand with his thumb. "Anyone who took me from you isn't worth my time and will not get my forgiveness."

"That include your parents?" I challenged.

"They know I'm here out of obligation, nothing more," he said as our waiter returned with a dish of the baked Alaska.

After pouring the liqueur over the top, our waiter lit it on fire, sending blue flames between us for a moment as the topping lightly browned and he passed us two forks.

"Thank you," I said, and he moved away. "I'm sorry I brought her up."

"Don't be," he replied. "I don't forgive, but I do forget. It's the only way I can survive most days. If I carried the weight of what I went through, I wouldn't be able to function. Trust me, I've worked programs, sat through therapy, and now, sitting across from you, I can restart the life I thought was gone."

We ate the dessert in silence, and after he paid, we got in the elevator to go the forty-plus stories down. He turned to me, took my face in his hands, and kissed me deeply, pressing me into the corner of the elevator, and I could taste the salt of his tears he'd been holding in that now streamed down his cheeks. When we both could feel the elevator slowing, he released me, turning away to wipe at his cheeks.

"You know we don't have—" I began as we walked to the car, and he cut me off.

"Yes, yes, we do," he said, pulling me into his arms. "You take away all of it."

"You're punishing yourself. You see that, don't you? By keeping yourself here with them."

"Then you came and found me, saving me from Hell." He brushed his lips across mine. "You feel it too, don't you? The calm between us. I've only experienced it with you. When I'd read and reread your letters, they were like bedtime stories to me, rocking me to sleep. Now with you here, all I can think about is being with you all the time."

"But we can't be together all the time."

"Only because I'd never ask you to give up the career you love," he said as his fingers stroked along my spine, sending tendrils of heat around my body. "Whatever you want from life, I'll be there to support you any way I can. Right now I can see the stress you're under by how you are at the end of the week. Why would I ever put added pressure on you by demanding the few minutes of free time you have at the end of the day?"

"Maybe a few minutes wouldn't be so bad," I reasoned, falling into an embrace that sent me over the moon as we slipped our way to his car, where I curled up next to him on the ride back to my place.

Chapter Nine

The sound of my zipper was followed by a kiss of cold from the cool air as we stepped into my home. Thankfully the click of my door relaxed me almost as much as the brush of Peter's lips along my neck. His fingers gently moved the sleeves of my nefarious dress down my arms, and then he marked a trail along the leisurely exposing flesh. Slowly he undressed me, his mouth peppering sweetness across my backside and down my thighs as my dress lowered to my ankles.

I let his hands lift one foot, then the other, to move the fabric past my red bottoms. For only a moment he left me, to drape my dress over the back of my couch, taking care in the action. Then the sapphire in his eyes returned as his hands found my hips once again.

"Almost perfect," he purred before kissing my lips and twisting his fingers around the strings of my thong. He lowered once again, this time leaving a trail through the center of my breasts, my belly, and finally kissing right above my sex as he repeated the action of keeping me steady as he moved the slip of fabric past my ankles. This he didn't use as much care with, tossing my panties to the side and gliding his hands along my legs to come to rest at my thighs. "Now I see perfection."

"You're a horrible flirt," I said.

He brushed his right hand along my shoulder, then down my arm, and moved it between the two of us, slipping one, then two, fingers between my wet folds. "Your lips can lie all you want, my sweet Divinity, but I have to say, I think you do it poorly."

He began stroking in and out, his thumb circling my clit at the same time. My knees started to give way, and I had to cling to him. I wrapped my arms around his neck as he removed his fingers from my aching pussy, causing me to whimper.

"Only a moment," he said before scooping me into his arms and carrying me to the second floor. I buried my head in his neck, kissing and sucking along it until I was placed on my bed and he climbed on top of me. Our tongues tangled between stripping off his sweater and shirt. When I reached for his waistband, he shook his head, his eyes dark with lust. "I didn't get the dessert I wanted."

Covering my smile, I watched as he descended down my middle, grabbed a pillow for under my hips, then devoured me with glee. My legs rested on his shoulders as I fell back, allowing him the banquet, with the mix of his tongue and fingers bringing me to orgasm as he suckled my clit to send me over the moon. Trembling and unsure I could keep my head, he led me after stripping off his slacks. He reached into my nightstand drawer to remove the condoms he'd placed there the weekend before, and I stopped him.

"We're not there yet," he said as he stood at the side of my bed, his erection hard, long, and at the perfect level to my lips as I shifted to sit.

"Oh yes"—I licked the salted slit at the tip—"we most assuredly are."

It was my time, time to settle the trembling in my core even if it was only for a moment. I licked along the thick vein under his shaft and curled my fingers around his hardness. Finally taking him in as far as I could, I allowed my hands to be the extra length required to cover him fully, pulling and sucking as he groaned above me. He rested his hands on my shoulders when his legs began buckling at the knees a bit, urging me on as he moaned.

"Jesus, Divinity, I thought your pussy was sweet, but your mouth is divine."

Increasing my speed, I circled his uncircumcised tip with my tongue, surely pulling back on the extra skin as I sucked in harder, and it hit the back of my throat. Tears began falling from my eyes, and my core betrayed me, tightening to the point another orgasm threatened to break. Between my hand and mouth, I could take in every inch of him, and when he tugged on my hair, I let out a hard breath, releasing him. Hot jets spurted across my bare breasts as he cried out, and I kept pumping with my hand until he was drained.

His mouth crashed down on mine, and we fell back onto the bed. My nails dug into his back for fear of slipping as he gasped above me. Eyes lightening, he captured my face in his hands.

"I don't think I've told you how much I love you," he said as he settled between my legs, "but tonight I'm going to show you. Let's get me off you in a shower. Then I'll be ready to ravage you correctly."

"Are we in competition to see who can please who the most?"

"I didn't think so," he said, "but it seems as if we might just be."

"I don't take losing well," I challenged.

"Me either, Motown."

We moved to the shower, where he placed my braids into my shower cap, tested the water before allowing me to enter, then proceeded to scrub me from top to bottom until the hot water ran out and he was harder than I thought physically possible. I also took care to lather and wash his chest, finding my way along the ridges of his tight abs with the same zeal he found with my curved ones.

"I never thought it was physically they meant when they say that a person is made for you, but have you noticed how well we fit together?" he said as the water cooled to lukewarm and he held me against him.

Turning off the water, I snuggled closer as the cooled temperature sent a little shiver down my back. Or was it the hardness now pressed between the two of us? Then again, his fingers were playing a number along my spine too.

"I'd given up my dream of the two of us," he admitted as if it were a sin, and he pulled one of the fluffy towels from the rack and began drying me off as he stood dripping. I would have done the same for him, but my arms were trapped behind terry cloth. "What about you?"

"The only thing I knew was you'd been sent away," I said, my head tilting a bit to the side. "I'd sent one letter, but it came back with a harshly written *return to sender* across your name, and I knew the one way I could reach you was gone. Even if I'd had your phone number, I'm sure I wouldn't have been allowed to talk to you."

"No." He tucked the towel in by my chest and pulled his own out. "And I never wanted you to feel my family's wrath."

"Was it simply a carnal desire sin keeping us apart?" I questioned.

"Pretty much. Dating was not really allowed in my house," he said. "At best, group gatherings were approved depending on who was there to supervise. Temptation was all around you, and if you didn't look out, you'd be pulled into the fiery pit of Hell."

"And yet—"

"I've already been to Hell, Divinity." He slipped off my shower cap and let my braids fall down to my shoulders. "Between your legs is Heaven, not Hell. If it is, then I could never judge the sinners of the world."

This time when we returned to my bed, we lay next to

each other, our fingers tracing the other's face as if we were memorizing for the time we'd need to be apart. That was my goal at least. His index finger glided over my bottom lip, slowly pulling us together, and when he rolled onto his back, I sheathed him in a condom before straddling his hips. I lowered myself over his shaft slowly, my thighs burning, but it was worth every lick of fire to watch the way his face shifted with each inch covered. Our eyes did not break from the other's. His hands resting on my hips didn't rush me. Instead they kept the slowness with each rock of my hips.

This was unlike any time we had been together. This was slow, sensual, with him sitting up to suckle my breast one moment and then our mouths coming together. Our touches were lovingly soft as we enjoyed being one and the same, not needing to say "roll right" or "left," "sit up," or "let me see" this or that. Communication came from the pleasure darkening his eyes, the way we bit our lips as the pace increased until we had to break apart.

His hand moved to my belly, then splayed wide as he moved up and covered my heart. The love deepened between us, and my want as well, as he kept me at bay even though his strokes were meeting the movements of my hips. Once again his hand moved to the back of my neck, this time bringing me down to his lips. He crushed me to him as we rolled, and he shifted my thigh, catching my knee at his elbow, widening me enough as my orgasm began building.

The speed and urgency finally took hold of both of us,

and I let him take me over the edge. Hard, demanding thrusts broke me apart until I was no longer in control, the feeling freeing to the point I was sure I was floating. Instead of fighting for command, I allowed the wave to crash into me as he praised me, and when my body fell apart, my core clenching him to the point he could no longer retreat from inside me, he instead ground against my clit.

"Fucking perfect," he purred in my ear. "Let go of me, sweet Divinity, and I will hold out until you've come a second time, I swear."

"You're acting...as if...I have control..." I gasped, my nails digging into his back. "If you move one centimeter, I will be done."

"A challenge," he said with a smirk before pulling back slowly, his cock dragging along my quivering walls. When he was almost fully out of me, his tip had to have hit my G-spot. Electricity surged through my body as he thrust deep inside, the pulsing along my walls sending frissons from the center to the very edges of my body and beyond.

In the morning I woke to an empty bed, wearing Peter's button-down shirt in the middle of rumpled sheets. I was pretty sure he must be around since I was wearing his shirt, but sadly, when I rolled over, there was a folded piece of paper on the nightstand simply saying *BRB, gotta get*

supplies. I smiled and was ready to roll back over when the doorbell rang. Thankfully I hadn't missed too much time with Peter. After running down the stairs, I was breathless when I opened the door wide to see Angela with a roller bag on the top step and Aaron on the sidewalk.

Slamming the door, I did my best to come down from my panic. What could I do at this point? I was half naked. *That doesn't mean anything. It's early morning, isn't it?* Shit, I hadn't put up a clock, and the sun was out. *No way I slept until noon, is there?* Heart thundering out of guilt, I opened the door slightly.

"Fuck you too," Angela said, then glanced over her shoulder to Aaron as I stood peering from behind the door. "Thank you, I'll deal with her now."

Aaron's poor fearful expression made me take pity on the kid as I gave a nod to dismiss him.

"Who was supposed to be on the other side of this door?" Angela accused. "I'm pretty sure I sent you a message last night telling you that agent booked me last-minute to fly down this morning and I'd be in before ten."

Pushing past me into my town house, Angela caught things I'd forgotten about. She kicked my discarded panties to the corner. Lifting my small purse, she removed my dead phone, which she tossed on the couch next to my dress.

"At least you didn't rip the seams," she said as her eyes went from my out-of-control braids to my bare toes, with an emphasis on the white button-down hanging to right above my knees. "This the pastor's? Or someone else you haven't told me about?"

"It's mine," Peter said from the doorway with a paper bag in one hand, wearing an old T-shirt I vaguely remembered from his car and the slacks from last night. "How many will there be for breakfast, Divinity?"

"Three." Angela spoke for me although she hadn't really acknowledged the man behind her as I struggled to find my voice. "Why your lips look like you've been sucking dick?"

"Angela," I admonished as heat threatened to have me bursting into flames at this point.

"Oh, you *can* speak."

Peter simply closed the front door and headed into the kitchen, giving me a light kiss on his way. "Breakfast will be ready in thirty minutes or so. I'll let you get your bestie up-to-date." He then whispered in my ear a warning that dropped my stomach. "I know when I left you weren't wearing panties. Has that changed?"

"Wait, he fucks *and* cooks?"

"Stop," I warned, making sure all the buttons were done on the shirt I was wearing.

"Oh no, don't cover up now," she said. "You, me, and poor little A-A-Ron know what happened in here already."

Storming up the stairs, I went in search of a pair of panties and shorts. I wasn't about to switch out of Peter's shirt. Smelling of his cologne was the only thing calming me in the moment. I breathed in from the collar as I went into my walk-in closet with Angela hot on my trail.

"Speak," she demanded.

"Yes, that's Peter, grown-up and—"

"Making breakfast after what I can only assume was a nefarious night," she said, stripping off her coat and tossing it on the bed.

"Far from it," I assured even though I could feel the lie on my tongue, and my bestie narrowed her eyes at me, demanding truths. "Okay, it was close."

"I kinda want all the details, but I think what's most important is, where has he been?" She crossed her arms. "Is he why I haven't been getting updates from you lately?"

"No, I've been working a lot," I said. "Since the first week, I've been getting my feet under me, and even he gave me space."

"Whatever has the girl who never sleeps past five in the morning getting up late?" She stopped to look at her charged phone for the time. "It's nearly eleven."

"I needed rest."

I did my best to catch her up on the hows and whys of what had happened to Peter. Most of it she bought, but I could see the doubting part of her popping up from time to time. Each objection I shut down while I twisted my braids up into a bun and got dressed.

"You're happy, I'm happy," she said. "Besides, I'm just dropping off my stuff here. I have a car coming in an hour to take me downtown."

"I'm surprised he didn't put you up in some five-star hotel."

"He would have," she replied with surety, "but I'd talked about you, and he was fine with getting me cars. Thankfully I found your little minion coming back from a run, and I asked if he knew Divinity Anderson. Guess he loves you, because he said, *'The woman I wish was my boss? She's in that town house.'*"

"Suck-up." I laughed, but couldn't help feeling a bit warm about him saying it.

"Breakfast," Peter called up to the two of us, and Angela pulled me into a hug.

"You brush your teeth," she teased me, and I smacked her since I actually had in the middle of the night.

"Ma'am."

"I'm not the one with swollen lips," she said. "Or were you doing that stupid thing with a bottle to try to make them Kardashian like?"

"Yes, yes, that's what I was doing all night," I replied, pulling on my house slippers, not about to divulge, although I knew eventually she'd break me.

"Is it as good as you remembered?" Angela nudged me with her shoulder.

"No," I sighed, trailing my fingers along the seam of his shirt.

"How you used to torture me with his skill, and you're telling me, now that you know how to fuck, it's bad?"

"No." I popped up from the bed. "It's ten times better, and I don't mean that because last night he gave me ten orgasms."

"He did not." She tossed a pillow at me, and I turned, using my ass to block it. "Preach, ma'am, preach."

Peter didn't miss a beat during breakfast, being his charming self as we ate biscuits and gravy. Angela informed him she gets boyfriend cooking rights. While she wasn't happy about the years between, the ease of the morning had her finally relaxing about him. He said he would let us have the day, but she told him it would be at least six before she'd back tonight.

"Then I can use and abuse you the way I wanted to," he said, curling his little finger around mine.

"Just wash the sheets. I didn't see a second bedroom upstairs." Angela's eyebrow raised. "And I plan on snuggling with my girl tonight."

"He wants me to rewire his house," I explained, though my sheets would need to be washed either way.

"Then do it, but drive your own car there. The three surefire ways to test a relationship"—Angela held up a finger and began counting off—"take a trip together, meet the parents, do a home renovation project. Basically, do it. That way you can end this before Divinity's heart is locked in. Took me years and a few frat boys to get her over you last time."

"Ignore her. She has head trauma that confuses her memory," I lied, and Peter brought the back of my hand to his lips.

"I'll take my chances," he said. "Besides, you can't keep living here. Elrod must be expecting you to get your own place, and mine is closer."

"Not to Detroit," Angela replied, and confusion furrowed Peter's brow.

My stomach tightened, having not discussed past the next few days with Peter. Much like he wouldn't make me give up my career, I couldn't imagine asking him to give up his parish. I just hadn't realized he thought I was moving down here. Thinking back, we'd had to balance between catching up and, well, falling into each other. The future was more about what hadn't happened than what would happen.

"You're not staying here?" he questioned as acid burned up from my chest.

"As of today, no."

"As of ever, no," Angela said, and I snarled at her. "Lie to him, but I know you. You are a Detroit girl through and through. This was a jumping-off point for you. Isn't this supposed to be a starting point for setting up plants globally?"

"Is it?" Peter asked.

The back of my neck burned, and my mouth became arid.

"I don't know," I replied honestly. "When I came down here, yes, it was what Angela said, a chance for me to prove myself for future projects. I'd be moved from running around the plant fixing errors to planning out new facilities and upgrading older ones."

"Why wouldn't you tell me that?"

"Why would you assume I'd be staying here?"

"Because you're building a plant. I didn't think that was a few-week commitment."

"Three months," I corrected. "I have three months to have it finalized. I've been coming back and forth down here for two years."

“What happens in two and a half months?” he asked, the question cutting through me like a freshly sharpened blade.

“She comes ho—”

“Don’t you have a car coming for you?” I bit, and Angela held up her hands in surrender as she backed out of the kitchen to where her luggage was. “Can’t we discuss this later, Peter?”

“I didn’t realize I was on a timeline.”

“We’re not in fourth grade anymore.” I took his hand in mine. “We have grown-up money, airline miles, and the ability to move wherever and whenever we want.”

“Angela forgot the fourth thing to destroy a relationship.”

“Don’t say it,” I warned, not about to hear how distance would pull us apart.

“Nosy best friends.”

I leaned over to him, our foreheads touching, before giving him a kiss. “Okay, you can say that.”

“We’ll figure it out, right?”

“Yes, and it doesn’t have to be today or even tomorrow.”

“Fine, but you’re still gonna rewire my house, right?” He scooped the last of the white sausage gravy up with a spoon and held it to my lips.

“No,” I said, and he shoved the spoon in my mouth.

“Sorry, couldn’t hear you. I’m pretty sure you said yum, but I was asking if we can rewire today?”

I shook my head, doing my best to swallow what was forced on me before answering. "No."

"Did I tell you my left ear doesn't hear as well as the right? Old baseball injury."

"No," I said again. Only this time he pulled me from the stool I'd been sitting on to his lap, tickling and kissing me until I gave in and cried out, "Yes, yes, okay, yes."

Angela's voice called out from the living room, "Was that number eleven?"

Chapter Ten

Dear Peter,

I should be mad at you, hold a grudge, and make you crawl on your knees to beg for forgiveness. At least that's what all the girls do on the TV shows I've been watching lately. I'm not sure why anyone would want to be with someone that treats them that way. Maybe I'm too nice. Angela says I am, but honestly, I missed you too. You're kind of my second-best friend. Go ahead, tell me your stories, but break them out over a few letters. I can't take twenty pages at once. Not since I got moved into honors math.

Some of those problems feel like a book with all the letters.

Vin

Dear Divinity,

I'll accept being your second-best friend, but I don't want to call you Vin. Your name is sunshine on a cloudy day. Yeah, you've got me loving Motown, the old stuff at least. Doesn't change the fact I like the way your name rolls off my tongue. Something tells me I'm not going to be able to get you listening to country. Maybe I'll give you my life story sometime. Right now I'm just having a difference of opinion with my father, and he's not a man you are allowed to have that with.

Everyone bows down to him as if God only listens to him on who is going to Hell. I don't believe in the fire-and-brimstone God. You can't be a loving God and one who punishes. Much like a parent that punishes a child for their own good. Maybe that kid needs to learn there is life on the other side of being bad, instead of always fearing being caught. He's not stopping me from wanting to fight Michael DeWitt when he runs his mouth and picks on the little kids. I still want to sneak a beer or kiss a girl. Well, not so much any girl, but dang it, maybe I should ball this up and toss it away. Then again, I'm in school, study hall, and there's a good chance it would be dug out of the garbage for my humiliation.

I bet you have a dozen boyfriends, a girl with eyes as dark as yours that somehow still sparkle. Maybe we shouldn't have started writing each other again. Or maybe my hormones are driving me crazy and I know you're the only girl I can really talk to. I'm not sure I'll be brave enough to send this, but if I do, Divinity, please answer it. Even if it's to tell me about the fifteen guys that have been fighting to take you out.

Your idiot,
Peter

"But did you kill him?" Angela questioned as we sat on my couch finishing off the obligatory meal when coming to Atlanta that I had so far avoided thanks to work: chicken and waffles from Gladys Knight's restaurant.

"No, I'd rather have a conscientious helper than one who guesses," I said, shifting the ice around my knee.

"And yet, you came home to me injured."

"He probably wishes I'd been more conscientious of the planks he'd taken out."

Peter was double-checking my instructions, and I'd turned to lay them out again when I stepped through the ceiling of the living room. The fuse box had been placed on the second level of the home, and I'd been working on checking the connections when it happened. Glad I wore my work boots and jeans to the home, but that didn't change the fact I'd wrenched my knee pretty well and even had scrapes through the jeans.

"Once I assured him I'd live, we both had a pretty hard laugh over it," I said. "You know, the embarrassing kind where you're practically choking."

"Did he kiss your boo-boo?" she teased while breaking off a piece of waffle and dipping it in maple syrup.

"None of your business. Now tell me about your day. Are you going to be a big-time TV star?"

"Maybe," she beamed, scrunching her shoulders together by her ears. "And maybe I'd be fine with you living in Georgia."

"Oh really."

"How many bedrooms does this man have at his house?" she joked. "And what's the closet space look like?"

"A really long commute if you're shooting a show in downtown Atlanta." Stretching out, I did my best to not bump my knee since I was working within the layout of the town house. "You should be rubbing my feet or something, shouldn't you? For being rude to me this morning?"

"I'm still eating."

"There isn't even any meat on those bones." I pointed to her chicken, then placed my foot in her lap. "We both know you crossed a line."

"But did I?" she questioned. "Because I'm thinking I was right to call you out, acting all crazy like you did something wrong."

"My subordinate was outside the door. I needed a minute."

"A-A-Ron, by the way, he thinks we're all weird in Michigan."

"Gee, I wonder why?" I mused, pointing my toes and circling my foot.

"You're lucky I love you," she said, rubbing on my foot, but when she hit my instep, I pulled back swiftly. We had been rubbing each other's feet for years, and suddenly it felt wrong, like this part of me was now for Peter—and only him. Never had I thought such a thing, and Angela was eyeing me warily. "Not that I'm complaining, because we both know I'm not about the manual labor, but ma'am, what the hell was that?"

"I don't know."

"Did he do kinky shit with your foot? Ewww, I touched that thing." She squirmed, wiggling her fingers like a magic spell to make my feet disappear.

"No, he didn't do kinky shit. He was babying me. Parts of me feel like his now," I explained, grabbing a throw pillow to yell into. "Why does life have to be hard? Why can't it be simple? I want him. He wants me. Why does there have to be other factors?"

"Let's see. It's not really a fairy tale, Vin," she said, stealing the last bit of waffle from my container.

"Then what's the point?"

"You know, I was thinking we should go check out this so-called church of his. I mean really find out what he's preaching there." She eyed me, and I waited for her go full-on teenager with a crazy plan. "We have time before my plane leaves tomorrow."

"Says the girl who counts running late as exercise," I chided, not about to tackle Sunday Atlanta traffic, dodging and weaving my way like a NASCAR driver because she's on a tight timeline.

"No, it's real this time. Joe wants me to have dinner with a few people from the studio. Then I'll fly home." She crossed her heart, but I demanded her phone and proof from her airline app. "I'm hurt. You act like I'm a liar."

"You have priors."

She tossed me her phone with the app open. My finger scrolled through her ticket as I verified the date and time because I couldn't believe she was putting herself out at all.

"You're doing a red-eye?"

"Not originally, but I slayed at the audition." Angela dusted off her shoulders like the badass bitch she was.

"Well, maybe we can go," I said, unsure about going when I hadn't been invited. Popping up at his job when he wasn't expecting it seemed wrong.

When we were working on his house earlier in the day, we avoided future talk. It was about now and nothing else. Too many factors were hanging unanswered for good reason. We were in a mix of old and new. Heartbreak would be hard, but Angela was right about one thing. If I was going to be with Peter, I needed to be all in, and right now we were playing at grown-ups just like when we were kids—dreaming of what could be, passing letters as if they were notes in school and he'd be able to respond in the next period, not the next week. All of it was now reality, and we couldn't simply use some origami and M.A.S.H. to determine our future.

"Don't suppose you brought a hat?" I questioned.

"Your damn heathen ass doesn't even understand that's an Easter thing," she snapped since she attended services in Detroit pretty regularly. "Some churches it may be more, but not in a small redneck town. These are salt-of-the-earth, hardworking folk."

Her mock voice had to be an imitation of some actor, but I couldn't place it, and I shook my head.

"You will need to update this mani and pedi," she said, taking in my nails, now completely destroyed thanks to having to do manual labor a bit too much lately. “Your hair, though, there ain’t enough time.”

“Has it grown out that much?” I’d gotten it done before Christmas and knew it needed tending. The night before I had taken a few braids to wrap around like a headband to cover the unbraided parts.

“Either that or Peter’s a tugger. Please say he’s a tugger. I shouldn’t like it, but damn, I do.”

“Like you need to live vicariously through me,” I said, and she gave me a shrug.

“Maybe I’m happy you’re finally happy. It’s not like you ran through men, but I saw you fake with Trevor and Terrence, both of which left you probably more in love with Peter. Either way I’m glad you never settled for Mr. Right Now.”

“Wait.” I sat up with my hands splayed out. “Are you finally on Team Peter?”

“He agreed to share you,” she said. “The others never even offered. Not once.”

The rest of the night I was caught up on the foolishness back home as we reverted to our ten-year-old selves doing makeovers. Searching for my basic nail supplies had been a feat in itself. Before we knew it, midnight passed, and Angela looked up the information for services. We saw only one was offered at eight a.m.

“What a jerk,” Angela said, then held her hand up. “Sorry, but not having two, like it’s so hard to talk to five people twice a day.”

“Looks like they have an active parish.” I took over her

phone and looked for pictures of him engaging with the community. "What do you think all this stuff is about?"

Angela peered over my shoulder and shrugged. Home-school links, praise services, there were activities every night of the week. No wonder Peter wasn't pushing hanging out after work. That's when he was hitting his stride. Poking on a page with the history, an image of his father and grandfather appeared with the years they were in service along with a story about the first Pastor Young founding the parish back around Prohibition.

"Seems like the Youngs have been being judgmental pricks since the dawn of time."

"Peter's not like that," I said.

"We'll see tomorrow."

I tossed and turned all night, and by the time I woke at six, I might have gotten a half hour of sleep. Even with Angela's mad makeup skills, I worried I wouldn't be presentable. If I showed up, was he going to introduce me to the parishioners? Fear tightened my tumbling belly, and all I could do was strangle my steering wheel as we made our way to the church. Angela sat yawning and occasionally messing with a braid that had fallen out of place. Once again I had made a headband with strands, but my hair was in a perfect bun. I wore a simple skirt and boatneck sweater, not low, but wide enough the simple chain I wore was on display, glinting in the winter sunlight.

Peter stood in a simple set of slacks, button-down, and a suit coat. Not exactly what I'd expected, but I did enjoy the fact he wasn't done up in adornments. He stood greeting people as they came in, but before we made it to the door, he was called away by a person Angela said was probably a deacon.

"Good morning, ladies." The man who'd sent Peter away extended his hand, and a young girl passed us each a pamphlet. "Haven't seen you here before, welcome, and please join us afterward for refreshments."

"Thank you," I said, bowing my head a bit, making Angela elbow me.

The church was deceptively big with a foyer opening up to a glassed-in sanctuary. Around the edges were rooms marked with words like *Nursery*, *Teen Challenge*, *Library*. Inside the sanctuary, three sections were set up, one directly facing the altar, the other two flanking at an angle.

"Okay," Angela said as we slipped into a side pew near the back, "I may have steered you wrong. I thought this was a little country church."

"We should leave," I replied, but she snatched my wrist and locked me in place. "There's a video screen, drum set, and electric guitars onstage."

"Maybe you're right, and Peter has shifted the message from what his father preached. And look at all the menfolk flocking without women locked on their arm."

"This is church, not an app where you can swipe right or left."

"And yet?" She nodded to a few men who were seated only three rows from the front.

The mix of ages, ethnicities, and, it appeared, financial

status was clear. Everyone was accepted in the space, making my heart warm.

“Do you think that’s appropriate?” a woman, not any older than I was, spat at me.

“I’m sorry, what?”

“That outfit you’re wearing? And you,” she added, nodding her head to Angela.

“I’m sorry, what? No, I’m perfectly fine, ma’am,” Angela said, and now it was my turn to keep her in her seat.

“Show much more flesh and I’m pretty sure Pastor Young will have a thing or two to say to the both of you.” Her pinched face had to hurt as she stormed away in her turtleneck and ankle-length skirt.

“Good thing the fashion police aren’t here, or there would be a ton of *whoop, whoop* sounds going on in here,” Angela said.

I began scanning the audience to see my bun probably wasn’t a problem, but the fact my clavicle showed might be. I glanced at Angela, who wore a high-neck shirt—but it had no sleeves—and dress pants, all perfectly normal and conservative, especially for her.

“I’m not sure I’m going to like this place,” I said.

Acid burned up my throat as the few men Angela had been making eyes at now focused on the front, where band members began arriving and playing in Peter. He walked down the aisle between our pews and the center ones, shaking hands with some, waving at others deeper in the rows. I made eye contact with him, but he seemed confused before getting onstage.

"We should go."

"No, we shouldn't." Angela was bouncing to the beat. "I'm not saying this is good music, but I've heard worse."

"Can I get an amen?" Peter called out

Everyone rose, most with their hands up, calling out, "Amen!"

I sat dumbfounded until Angela smacked my shoulder and I shot up, doing my best to reply at the right time to his second and third call of amen.

"Bless us, Jesus, and those who do not know their sins, let them find you," Peter said, earning him an instant amen from the crowd. "Y'all know I normally let the band play and all of you sing, but today I can't do it."

"Why not?" a man called out.

"I'll tell you why not, Bill. It's because of witches, witches that try to steal your soul, and I can feel they've been coming in our church, our place of worship." Peter's ire rose and rose as his cheeks flushed bright red. "Satan has been sending his demonic whores to our safe haven, and let me tell you, I'm not going to allow it. Come in here without Jesus in your heart, and I'll send you right back out."

"Amen, amen," the crowd cheered, a fevered pitch rising in the room, and I could feel gooseflesh burning from the knitted fabric covering me.

"What in the hell?" Angela said under her breath.

"I'm telling you demonic whores have come to our sanctuary, but I see you. I always see you, and I'm going to tell you one thing." Peter's finger pointed directly at me. "Not with my flock you won't."

The parish turned, but faced a young woman sitting three rows up from us. Her face turned crimson as she tried to pass off his accusatory point as being for someone else before she began crying. Two men came down the side of the aisle and dragged her from the building, her cries for forgiveness echoing in the room until Peter held his hand up and asked for a moment of silence to pray.

"That shit just happened," Angela said. "Like seriously just happened. What the hell?"

"What the hell indeed." I stared at Peter as he rolled into another rant about some sort of sin taking over the place and challenged those present to call people out. My stomach bubbled and churned, and I knew I had to leave, or I would lose every part of what I knew to be true.

I slid down the pew to get to the end, but a man sat down, blocking me. When I turned, it was Peter, my Peter, not the man on the stage spewing hate, but the man I'd fallen in love with. Only how?

"There's something I haven't told you," he said as my head kept on a swivel looking between him and...well, him.

"Let's get out of here before the crowd really turns," Peter said, and I stared at him, unsure which would be worse:

stay for the sermon of hate or go with a man I now knew nothing about. "Divinity, you know me."

"No, obviously I don't." I pushed past him and ran out the door to the sounds of whoops and hallelujahs as if the man onstage had been successful in casting out the Devil herself.

The world around me spun, and no matter how deeply I breathed in the air, I couldn't find it. I was drowning in the middle of a parking lot. No water, simply lies and confusion and an unwillingness of my body to come to rights with itself. *No, I don't do this*, I thought as blackness started to come in around the edges of my vision. *I don't swoon, or faint, or find weakness others have all the time.* I was strong, independent, and obviously not in need of a man.

"Angela, you drive," I said, opening up my car door and crashing into the passenger seat.

When the car didn't instantly move, I searched for her, my view a mix of waves as if I were in the desert and heat was creating illusions. That was it. The Peter onstage was an illusion. Or was the one sitting next to me a fantasy I'd conjured up to figure out what was happening to the world falling apart around me?

Trevor and Terrence had never had my heart, but obviously they were a pattern. One from which I hadn't escaped. I'd convinced myself that well-written words were who Peter was instead of seeing the true him, the one whose jaw ticked when I called him by his name as if that were wrong. He never asked to be called Pete, Petey, or even

P-dog like some ignorant child. At best he'd sign his letters with a simple P instead of forging his brother's signature. Nothing more, nothing less. I'd romanticized his love of letters instead of seeing the man afraid of his shadow casting out aspersions to everyone else.

Why had I let the words where he said his father was a failed man for preaching fear convince me of his good? The arms that surrounded me had silenced arguments I would have had about him. Should have had about him. Unlike those who had come before, I didn't allow them voice. No, *he* didn't. How could I have been so enraptured to not see what was blatantly before me? More importantly, where the ever-loving fuck was Angela?

Opening the passenger door, I heard her yelling.

"You stay the fuck away from her," she warned.

"I just need to explain," original Peter said.

"Not today, not tomorrow, and how about never again?"

"She'll understand, I swear."

"Vin told me to drive," Angela snapped. "Me. To quote my girl, bumper cars aren't roadworthy. But I'm going to drive her as far and as fast away from your ass as I can."

The driver's side door opened, and she got in and pressed the ignition button as Peter ran in front of my car and placed his hands on the hood. "Divinity, I need to explain."

His eyes implored me, cutting through the windshield and driving straight into me. My hazy world suddenly had sharp straight lines as I made out the face of what should have been my future. The sound of the GPS acquiring the map hummed in my ears.

"He's my brother," he said. "He's Peter. I'm Paul. He stopped writing you, but I didn't want to lose your voice."

Angela gave him one beep in warning. He jumped back a bit, then came to my side of the car, but she locked the door to keep him away. I could only hear him through glass.

"Look forward, Vin," she said.

"It's only a name. I'm the person you fell in love with, me!" he cried out right before she peeled out of the parking lot.

If Angela was talking, I didn't hear her. His final words, *"I'm the person you fell in love with,"* were running on repeat over and over. Paul? Peter didn't have a brother. Only parents, nothing more. No siblings. But they were too similar to not be related. Jesus, who the hell was he? I sat in my thoughts for about five minutes, until she started tapping my arm and the road became bumpy.

"Vin, Vin, I need you to snap out of it for like thirty seconds. Then you can go back to your own personal *Twilight Zone*," Angela said. "I don't remember there being a gravel road, but this is where your car told me to go."

I'd been lost in the pines alongside of the road. It wasn't until the field opened up that I saw Peter's home, the one his uncle had left him and the one I'd rewired and watched as he worked on patching up holes the day before.

"Why did you bring me here?" I snarled.

"I didn't bring you anywhere. I hit home, and it went here," she said, coming to a stop by the front door, where a porch had been framed in.

Getting out of the car, I tried my best to breathe in the fresh air and go back even an hour in time, when it would have been okay to go to the wrong place, because it wasn't wrong, it was all kinds of right. Sitting on the top step of the treated wood, I settled in and glanced around the property, to the place where I'd made love to him. I couldn't say his name. He no longer had one I could comprehend. He was a nameless thing.

"What is this place, Vin?" she asked.

"Pe—his house, the one I rewired yesterday. He's renovating the place after his uncle left it to him. He talked about moving in now he could see beyond tomorrow." Dropping my face into my hands, I shook out my shock and stood in bemusement. "It's official. I have a broken picker."

"I don't think so," Angela said as she sat next to me.

"Are you on his side?"

"Hell no. You know I'm down for you like four flat tires. I made him give me the ten-second explanation."

"What did he mean his name is Paul?" I asked.

"Twins," she said. "Basically, Peter stopped writing, and Paul took over."

"Then who did I fall in love with? Did they switch? Were they both playing me? Who did I have sex with?"

"Well, the one who kept talking about a whore in the sanctuary might be a clue."

"Fuck you," I spat, but I needed her sarcasm and wit to keep me balanced.

"Ten seconds, that's all I gave him."

"And?"

"I'm really not sure what you expect me to say," she said. "You know I'm all about the tea, and right now, all I want to know is what the hell is happening. This is better than a reality TV show."

"It's my life."

"And that sucks for you, but I didn't get to weave snatch the bitch in the church, so you have to give me something."

"Are you serious? Why am I your friend?"

"Remember the bad back and dead bodies?"

"A twin?"

"Yeah, it's like *Guiding Light*, *Young and the Restless*, and *All My Children*."

We sat for what seemed like forever, or as long as Angela could handle not talking, which meant forever to her.

"Not wanting to be all about me—"

"Since when?" I teased, unsure if the stabbing pain in my eye was a headache or migraine.

"Love you too," she said. "Can I point out hard liquor is at your house?"

"Fine."

This time I drove. Knowing my address, I got home and went straight to my room. There wasn't much else I could do at this point. Angela brought me water and a box of Cheerios.

"I can skip my meeting," she offered, but it was empty since she knew there was no chance I'd stop her from taking over the world.

"I'm good. I've gotten a few texts from Devin, so I'll work," I said, sliding my laptop from beside my bed and powering it on. Emails, texts, and a dozen other spec layouts kept me distracted until Angela came up to say good-bye. We locked pinkies and pressed our foreheads together.

"I can't believe I'm saying this, but let him explain," she said. "Your picker isn't broken. I promise it isn't."

"Great, now I don't know my best friend or boyfriend. Did I even wake up this morning?"

"You did. I know you won't want to hear this, but I've never seen you happier than over breakfast yesterday," she said. "He did that. Whatever-his-name-is was who did that."

Once I heard the door click, I went to the closet, pulled out the box of letters, and tried to find where Paul began and Peter disappeared. The handwriting was slightly different, but age could have done that. Mine went through its own transformation over the years. Either way, at what point was this façade going to change? Was I supposed to find out when we moved in together? Got married? Whenever it was, I couldn't understand why he didn't simply tell me.

Chapter Eleven

The next morning I did my best to keep my pissy attitude at bay. Looking at Aaron when he dropped off a package wasn't going to happen. All I could do was focus on my work and get to five o'clock. Harmony was busy, as interviews were in full swing, and if she wasn't greeting a new person, she was escorting another out or answering questions from the person sitting in the chairs.

When I swore it had been five hours, but was really only thirty minutes, I went in search of my meter. In order to make sure the connections were done right, I needed to do checks. My irritation was at ninety as I began slamming drawers after the first three had no glory.

"Hey, Ms. Anderson, is there something I could help you find?"

"My meter," I bit, then held up a hand to apologize. "I'm sorry I snapped. I know where I left it, and someone moved it. But did they put in a place where it belongs? No."

"I did," she said, placing a delicate hand on my wrist. "I put it on the charger under your desk."

Embarrassment heated my cheeks. "Like I told you to on Friday." I nodded my head. "Again, I apologize."

"You were running out of the office. I'm not surprised you forgot."

"Doesn't mean I have the right to yell at you," I said.

"You weren't yelling, trust me. Any chance you were able to tell that guy sorry from the delivery chick?"

"I did. He wasn't interested. By the way, did you know a guy named Paul Young?"

"Peter's brother?" Harmony nodded. "Of course, he was legendary for a bit, until his parents wouldn't let him go to a farm league at seventeen and he gave up baseball altogether."

"Why wouldn't they?"

"He's the younger twin. He was supposed to understudy his brother, your friend Peter."

"I'm not really sure he's my friend."

"Oh, okay. Well, I put your letter in your desk drawer, seemed a little personal to be sitting out."

"My letter?" I questioned.

"Yeah, some old one with a post office sticker to return to sender."

A chill rippled through me. Did I dare read a letter I knew was Paul, not Peter? It was the only one I knew for certain came from him.

"Thank you, I'd forgotten about it."

I headed back to my desk, reached under, retrieved my meter, then slid the thin desk drawer where I had pens, pencils, and generic supplies. Lying on top of an unopened pack of sticky notes was the yellowed letter. When I took it from the drawer, I could feel the heft in my hand. It wasn't a simple postcard-length letter. Paul was talking to me for real, and he'd given this to me almost two weeks ago.

My finger glided underneath the barely sealed envelope, and I pulled out a still white sheet of paper. No lines, this was proper stationery. When I unfolded the trifold paper, a picture fell to my desk. A smiling Paul beamed in the middle of a group of six men, his hair shorn pretty short and a beard longer and unruly. The 4" x 6" candid was from his life beyond the bounds of his father. It may have been his punishment, but Paul turned it into his salvation.

Dearest Divinity,

I saw you today. You didn't see me. I couldn't step to a woman practically glowing with a man on her arm. Not when she was meant to be mine. Circumstances brought us together and tore us apart. Only you don't know the full story of how we came together, and you deserve to know.

Back in fourth grade, you returned a

letter to Peter Young, my twin brother. Bet you didn't know Peter had a brother. I figured it out pretty quickly he never told you about me. Not surprising. Our parents should have named us Cain and Abel, not Peter and Paul. That doesn't explain us coming together.

He is the one you wrote for class. He wrote you a few times after the assignment. I got Lonny Vacini, and I'm pretty sure the kid couldn't spell, let alone write a coherent sentence. When Peter would finish with your letters, he'd toss them aside, and I'd pick up the toss-offs. He did want to be your friend initially. I don't want you to think any different. But we went to camp one summer, first baseball, then Little Shepherd. I'm sure you know which one I did better at. He took the word and need for us to stay away from girls a bit too serious.

You'd sent one letter randomly, and I got home before he did. I know it was crazy, but you were having a time, and I needed to reply to the beautiful girl in the picture upset about not seeing her parents. I was the other side of the coin. I wanted to do anything I could to avoid mine. When I got to the end of the letter, I sat for an hour unsure what to do. The letter was personal to me, about me, but I'd noticed over the years from the few letters I'd read after Peter, you never asked about me. It was then I knew he never mentioned me. Not once.

How could I say this is Paul, not Peter? You'd think your friend was a schizoid or something. I feared losing the only connection with you. This is why I never wanted you to call. You'd ask for Peter, and either you'd think you'd gone crazy or be confused, and I wanted to tell you in person. All of it was a mask to hide myself behind, but with each letter, we both came to a point I wasn't sure I could walk away from. Only my lie had become my life, worse, my nightmare.

When we finally met, I tried, I swear I did, but what happened between us was beautiful, and I knew I had to tell you. It wasn't a question, you thought you'd made love to Peter. You knew me, not my name.

That is all. The rest was me. From almost the beginning to what became the end.

Only I had held out hope, selfishly, that I would find my way back to you. Never thinking about you moving on in the way you must have, because I couldn't. You had become my only thought, and now it will be the punishment my father said I deserved.

I hope you are happy and found your way. If there comes a time you want to talk, I will always be there for you. Always, for you have been the light in the darkness, the quiet in my storm, and if there is a chance for the two of us, know I will be yours forever.

Paul the fearful fool

Rereading the letter a dozen times wouldn't make it clearer to me. I would have understood, wouldn't I? My early letters had a bit of me revealed, nothing major, but my later ones were practically diary entries. I wasn't sure I could have accepted or even understood then, because right now, I couldn't see past the folded letter sitting idle on my desk.

When the door opened, I expected to see another interviewee. Instead either Peter or Paul walked in, and Harmony nodded toward my desk. I sat paralyzed as he took steps toward me. Each one made it harder to breathe until I was back underwater and drowning on land.

"Can we go somewhere and talk?"

"I'm not supposed to go places with strangers," I said, gasping a bit, which took the bite out of my retort.

"Lunch? First date?"

"I don't remember swiping right on a dating app." Even I could hear the tremble in my voice and feared what would happen if I crashed into the wall I'd created instead of stepping through the door.

"Motown, I dug myself into a hole I couldn't get out of," he said, and the sweet moniker he used when not being sexual, but my friend, triggered my need to know more.

"You've got five minutes, outside." I got up with my meter so I could go to work after.

"More than I deserve," he said as we walked out and over to the side of the trailer.

"Speak." Keeping my arms crossed, my jaw ticked, and I kept my eyes down knowing how those crystal blue beauties would take me over in a heartbeat.

"I fucked up."

"You didn't trust me," I spat, then held up a hand. "Sorry, continue."

"I liked you from the first letter. My brother shared the responses. He made fun of me for having a moron to write to. Of course, a girl named Divinity was a sign according to my father." I watched as his feet kicked a bit at the gravel. "When you told how you got the name from your grandmother, between your curl of hair and love for the sweet treat, Peter started to become disenchanted."

"And you?"

"Liked you even more. When you sent that first picture, all I saw was the light in your eyes."

Looking up, I cursed myself. Damn vanity making me show off what he said he liked. As expected, he took a step and cupped my chin in his hand, my body betraying me once again as it softened, knowing the feel of him and craving the absence.

"It's a name," he said.

"It's a lie," I countered.

"But is this?" He leaned down and captured my lips.

The smell of his cologne, feel of his familiar lips had me falling into where and how we'd been. He was right, and I hated him for it. I didn't want to like him, let alone love, but I couldn't change the way we were together. It was more than a simple childhood infatuation. We were more than lust-driven lovers.

"I need time," I said, backing away from the invisible hold he had on me. "I hear what you're saying, but what if Angela had taken over writing you?"

"What if you signed Angela, but told me every bit of truth about you? That is what happened. I love you, Divinity. I fell in love with the girl who wrote personal words to me and held me in that camp all those years ago. Only my signature was a lie. Everything else was true."

"Until you want to switch places with your brother? You stay in Billingsworth."

"I stay because my mother cannot handle my father's dementia. He gets violent when confused. My brother sees him as a prophet, needing his approval all the time, but not willing to do the heavy lifting around being a caretaker. The only reason I was in the church is because my father insists on going."

"You brought your parents?"

"Yes, and I stand outside until the damn mockery is over," he explained. "I saw you and was on my way to the back when my brother started in on a diatribe."

"What do you do if you're not at the church all day and night?"

"I'm a carpenter and handyman around town," he said. "Suck at electrical, though."

"Then your life is in Billingsworth until your father passes," I surmised.

"There are a few on the board wanting to oust my brother. I might end up being a pastor. The kind I talked about."

"Really?" With how much hate he had in the letters growing up, I wondered why he would be interested in such a thing.

"My time in Central America did change me a little," he said. "I love where I grew up. But if you go back to Detroit, I'll sell my house and make the move."

"What if I don't want you in Detroit?"

"Then I'll have to try to convince you the man you fell in love with is far from a saint, but he's a good man, with a heart that has only and will only belong to you."

Epilogue

Dear Henry,

I never thought I would have to write a letter like this. I feel as if I'm failing my second father, but much like my father, I'm hoping you'll understand this is what will make me happiest. Besides, we both know I love a challenge, and what could be more challenging than working with slightly touched savants like the ones I've found in Georgia?

Maybe my life will free me up to be a project manager again, but this new line of electric cars the plant will be producing will keep me challenged enough for right now.

Plus, I've found a community here unlike any I knew in Detroit.

Yours Sincerely,
Divinity Anderson
Manager, Electrical Division, Elrod Motors
Bended Brooke Plant

Paul had brought back my love of letters. When the plant was up and running, I'd asked if I could stay on an extra three months, only to be offered the next plant project when I'd hit the six-month mark of living in Georgia. My turning down the promotion should have been emailed, but I wanted the personal touch for a man who'd been my mentor. The next letter he got would be an invitation to my marriage with Paul in the fall.

While he would never take over his father's church, enough people left when he offered to start another. It wasn't exactly what I'd expected, but they weren't the typical three-meetings-a-day type of place. It was a respite for many who'd been shunned from his family's church. In a way, he helped me find my own spirituality, not because I was engaged and would be a pastor's wife, but because he'd taught me God would embrace me how I came to him. How we all came to him. Broken or whole, hiding scars or wearing them proudly. Exactly how he was in the letters, minus his name.

The more I learned about Peter, I understood why Paul bristled every time I called him by the wrong name. While I was sad to lose the vision of the man named Peter I'd cherished, the man named Paul more than made up for it. To me, Peter was like meeting a celebrity only to find out they're an asshole.

"Quick question," Paul said as he held me from behind in bed. "How much trouble would you be in if you called in sick?"

"Thought you weren't going to stop me from taking over the world."

"I'm not, just asking for five minutes." He kissed the back of my neck.

"Five minutes?" I questioned as my arm snaked around to cradle his head. "The last time you kissed me there, I didn't see sunlight for three days."

"Lies," he grumbled, kissing along the column of my neck. "You may not have left the bedroom for three days, but I know the curtains were open."

"That's what it was," I said, being tempted by his gentle kisses slowly shifting into rough. "Either way, it's my first day as the big boss lady, and you know the boys aren't happy."

"Aaron is," he purred along the curl of my neck. "Should I be jealous of his hero worship of you?"

"Yes, when I get home, be prepared to worship me properly." I slipped away from him as the sun began cresting over the pines outside of our home. Slight shadows fell perfectly as he lay on our pale yellow sheets, part of the bright coloring I'd incorporated into the home as I made it ours. It was open for visitors, including a crazy best friend who now required guest room benefits at least twice a month. Angela wasn't going to buy a condo in downtown Atlanta since I wasn't available for nefarious nights anymore. No, she wanted to be close for her intended auntie duties.

All of which would come when God planned it. Right now we were putting a house together. Much like our relationship, from the outside there were holes, problems, and death traps, but the foundation was strong, and a love like ours could never be named.

Excerpt of No Weapons by L. Loren

LONG RANCH SERIES

GLORIA

"Welcome to Pastor Morgan Twomey's anniversary celebration! The doors of the church are open. Our beautiful First Lady is at the altar accepting your love offerings. Make your way down front and show pastor how much you care."

Deacon Barnes stood on the pulpit making the welcome address for my husband's twentieth anniversary as the pastor of New Birth Missionary Church. Standing there in my pristine white suit, I plastered on a fake smile and greeted the congregation. Afterall, it was my sworn duty as the wife if this religious man.

My father had groomed me to be the perfect First Lady and I could never say no to Daddy. Only he was no longer on this earth, and I was allowing myself to feel my true feelings. I didn't want to be here on a Sunday evening waiting for people to hand me envelopes of money that I would never get to spend. Morgan would snatch up this cash as soon as the benediction was said.

I also had no desire to greet these heffas who smiled in my face and seduced my husband behind my back. It was well known in the Charlotte church circles that my husband was a philanderer. People talked about us behind our backs, but still came to church religiously every Sunday morning. Word was they were waiting for drama to ensue, but I didn't plan to entertain them no matter what came my way.

Truthfully, I was feeling out of sorts all day. My stomach had been doing flip flops since I opened my eyes this morning. I chalked it up to me missing my baby girl. She was usually with me at these events. Yesterday, her father and I drove her to her new home in Atlanta for the next four years. I was a little scared to leave my child in that run down dorm, but my husband convinced me it was all a part of the college experience. Against my better judgement, I left my baby girl at Spellman College. She would get the chance to discover who she wanted to be in this world. It was more than I ever got from my father.

The music from one of my favorite songs by Mary Mary rang out into the sanctuary. The ladies were very talented singers, so I always enjoyed their rendition of the song. Before the choir uttered the word 'shackles', my attention was drawn to a very pregnant woman. For some unexplained reason I couldn't take my eyes off her, as she waddled her way toward me.

The pink dress she was wearing snaked up her thighs as she came closer. My body became hot, and it felt like a hot flash was starting. Not now, Lord. This menopause was not for the weak. I could have sworn the scent of ash wafted from the woman the closer she got to me.

A squeaky-clean smile marred her face as we made eye contact. It was meant to put me at ease, but it missed its mark. Something evil was present in this holy place. Well, as holy as a church could be with a pastor who regularly broke his marriage vows.

"Good evening, First Lady. I hope this will bless you and pastor Twomey," the woman said as she extended a pink envelope towards me.

Reluctantly, I took the offering from her, careful not to touch her hand. I saw right through this demon. She was up to no good and wanted to play in my face as her plan came to fruition.

"God bless you, Sister?"

I formed it as a question because I had no idea who this woman was. She wasn't a member of the church because I knew everyone. The congregation was growing, but I did my best to keep up.

As is tradition in our church, I opened the envelope to reveal her gift. In less than a minute, my entire world was shaken. As soon as the seal was broken on the envelope, a bunch of pink confetti popped out as a pre-recorded voice cheered 'It's A Girl!' The choir stopped singing and the room went silent.

The announcement startled me so much that I dropped the pink monstrosity causing a large sonogram to fall onto the floor. I wasn't daft enough to miss what this woman was trying to tell me. When I looked up at Morgan, his face told me everything I needed to know.

That's when I realized that the smell of ash wasn't my imagination. It was the smell of the burning tea leaves from the hot gossip this woman was itching to spill. A wicked smile spread across her face as she appeared to be waiting to see what I would do. Well, if she was waiting for a reaction from me, she wasn't going to get one.

Straightening my posture, I snagged my purse from the nearby table. I lifted my head, like the queen I am, and marched down the aisle making sure to step on the dreadful sonogram on the way out. I could hear Morgan calling after me, but I kept walking. This was the last straw.

Books by Michel Prince

Long Ranch Series

"Cowboys and love mixing it up."

One Last Rodeo-Novella

One Last Sunset ****

The Last to Know

The Last Laugh

At Long Last

Chrysalis Series

"The hardest part of growing up is learning you are worth more."

Chrysalis*

The Beam

Not Even Death

Unto Us

The Growing Strong Series

"Biology is the last thing that makes a family."

The Guardian's Heart**

The Queen's Heart

The Politician's Heart

The Teacher's Heart

The Frozen Series

"If your heart is frozen in time, can it still beat?"

Shared Redemption

Redemption of Blood

Stolen Redemption

Love by the Yard Series

"Tackling love one down at a time."

First and Ten

Second and Short

Third and Long

Fourth and Goal

Encroachment

Steel MC Montana Charter Series

co-authored with Wren McCabe

"Steel sharpens Steel."

Roadkill

Lil' Mama

Preacher Girl

Lil' Bit

Free

Cream

Dreamer

Topaz

Nightingale

Doc

Turbo - ###

Steel MC- Origins Charter

co-authored with Wren McCabe

Encased by Steel

Cloaked by Steel- Coming Soon

Concealed by Steel- Coming Soon

Healed by Steel-Coming Soon

Permanent Hangover Series

Two Ink Minimum

Ink All Night

Mixed Ink

An Enchanted Bedtime Story

Fairytale Retellings

Stalked-Jack and the Beanstalk

A Need So Great-Rapunzel – Coming Soon

Aberration Series

The Amalgam #

The Shield

The Seer

The Soul Reader

RYD Series

At Her Service ##

Fully Covering Her

The Ojeda Chronicles

Amara Acquired

Love on the Run

Always a Groomsman

Sin City MC-Multi Author Series

Ice

Fubar

Getaway Chronicles –Multi Author Series

Tempered Beats

Preacher's Kid Series- Multi Author Series

Divine Embrace

Stand-Alones

Silly Girl**

Unwrapping a Marriage-coauthored with Reana Malori*****

Mask of Fire

Kiss from a Rose

Triple B Baking Co-First Book in Hearts of Braden Series

Hollywood Lights, Austin Nights-Hell Yeah Kindle World

Muted Swan-A F'd Up Fairy Tale

By the Light of a Blizzard

Joyful Kitty

The Rotation

Love in the Land of Lakes- An anthology-Her Stranger

Festivals of Love-An Anthology-Tightly Wound

Beyond a Moment-Loving Hearts Anthology

*Winner 2014 Sweetest Romance IRAE

**Nominated for Book of the year 2013 LASR

***Nominated for a RONE 2014

**** Nominated for Best Contemporary IRAE 2015

***** Nominated for Summer Indie Book Award 2017

Finalist for MN Book of the Year 2022- YA

Finalist Imajinn Award 2022- Romance

5 Star Reader's Favorite Rank

###-Finalist Heart Award 2023 from Oklahoma Romance Writer Guild

Coloring Book

Love in Every Shade

Stay up-to-date with the author, sign up for her newsletter:

Website:

www.MichelPrinceBooks.com

TikTok:

https://www.tiktok.com/@michelprincebooks?is_from_webapp=1&sender_device=pc

YouTube

https://tinyurl.com/yccqt593

About the Author

USA Today Bestselling author, Michel Prince, graduated with a bachelor's degree in history and political science. Michel writes New Adult and adult contemporary, paranormal and Sci-fi romance as well as Young Adult adventure.

With characters yelling "It's my turn damn it!!!" She tries to explain to them that alas, she can only type a hundred and twenty words a minute and they will have to wait their turn. She knows they'll eventually find their way out of her head and to her fingertips and she looks forward to sharing them with you.

When Michel suppresses the voices in her head, she can be found cheering for her son in a variety of sports. She owes a huge thanks to her family for always being in her corner and especially her husband for supporting her every dream and never letting her give up.

Michel was awarded Elite Status with Rebel Ink Press in 2013, the service award for her local RWA chapter Midwest Fiction Writers in 2013 and 2014, and Sweetest Romance at IRAE 2015. In 2022 she was a finalist for Minnesota Book of the Year for Young Adult, a Finalist for

Best Romance in the Imajinn and a 2023 Finalist for Heart Award.

She resides in the Twin Cities with her husband, son, and dogs, Bolt and Sawyer.

www.ingramcontent.com/pod-product-compliance
Lightning Source LLC
LaVergne TN
LVHW010058170826
845678LV00012B/2170

* 9 7 8 1 9 9 8 3 5 9 0 1 1 *